THE ROAD TO SURVIVAL

DRIVING FORCE: BOOK 3

GREG CHASE

BAYOU MOON PUBLISHING, LLC

Copyright © 2021 by Greg Chase

First Edition 2021

Cover Art by Ravven

Editing by Angie Ramey

ISBN print: 978-1-953422-39-2

Bayou Moon Publishing, LLC

ABOUT THIS BOOK

The Road to Survival Blurb

Swash Jones and the crew of the Beast have made their exit from Warlord Inferno's camp. The respite from their troubles gained them useful information that will help them survive. That's the good news. The bad is that they lost Blade, their weapons master, which leaves them vulnerable. Too vulnerable. And with their nemesis, Scorch, out for revenge, Swash is going to have to keep a careful watch to avoid falling into a trap.

To continue Whisper's mission of locating the key master, however, means straining his overburdened crew to the breaking point. Though Swash is willing to endure both physical and mental assaults, Whisper must confront her very essence.

If the girl can reconcile the differing aspects of what

makes her unique, Swash and his crew just might find the answers humanity needs to survive.

_S_wash Jones aimed the roof-mounted floodlights of the earth rover, Beast, between a pair of long-dead pine trees. Ahead and below them, the lights illuminated a dried lake bed. Horizontal white, black, and gray lines bisected the rock pinnacles as testament to the lake's failed struggle to survive. He shut down the twin multifuel engines at the edge of the gray clay. "What do you think?"

Roach was busy studying Whisper's antique map which had been drawn when the basin was still filled with water. "Though it looks solid, there's no telling how soft that ground might be. I'd hate to get our tires bogged down in whatever muck might be lurking under the thin layer of dried silt."

The mechanic's assessment was in line with Swash's hopes. "This might not be the best camping spot, but if the ground is unstable, no one will be sneaking up on us through that canyon."

In the green glow of the light that illuminated the map, Roach's gen mod monkey ancestry showed in the thin lines of his jaw, cheek, and forehead. He looked up from his studies. "I doubt the ground would be the greatest deterrent. According to the topographical chart, we're right smack in the middle of the vector zone. No one's going to risk the death plague by traveling through this area."

Swash appreciated Stitch's efforts at warding off the pathogens that threatened every step they took outside of the Beast, but what she could do others could as well. "That's assuming we can trust that germaphobe biochemist not to reveal his secrets—or hand a case of inoculants to Scorch as a way of getting back at us."

Roach shrugged his narrow shoulders. "We can only stay one step ahead for so long. Eventually our advantage is sure to diminish. Best we can do is use what time we have to our advantage." He activated the dashboard holographic image that the long-distance hawk drone was capturing four miles ahead and nearly a mile up. The large satellite dish on the hill across from the lake bed was streaked with ash. It looked to be abandoned. "Your call, boss."

There really wasn't much to decide. Swash had already given his word to Whisper that they would keep looking for her illusive key master. "Wake up your girlfriend. You might as well call Stitch to the bridge as well." Being down a weapons master made Swash double-check their surroundings. The wide swath of downed trees, flattened by the Beast's eight-foot-diameter tires, led a path straight to them through the dried dead trunks. To properly protect their rolling habitation, Swash needed a larger crew. Instead, he was going to have to divide his precious force in two.

After hitting the wake-up alerts to both berths, Roach returned to drone control. Rotating the hawk around the top of the mountain provided a 360-degree hologram of the installation. The rendering was just gaining high-definition as Whisper entered the bridge in her nightgown. "How far away is it? Can we go there now? Why are we just sitting here?" The questions tumbled out of her mouth like she couldn't control her thoughts.

"Four miles ahead and one mile up," Roach said. "The Beast is going to have one hell of a time getting through the terrain. Getting her stuck in the mud at night isn't going to make for a stealthy approach."

"Even if we made it across," Swash continued, "we'd alert anyone manning the mountaintop controls."

Whisper nodded and took the center observation chair. "Are there even any signs of life?"

Roach spun the drone to catch any movement on the ground below. "Not in the compound, but there are some caves below the ridge. I didn't want to poke around too close in case someone was watching." The drone view screen highlighted a handful of large openings in the rocks.

Swash pointed at the largest cavern. "That's probably part of an old mining operation. These mountains are riddled with caves. After the wars, a lot of these holes were turned into subterranean living spaces to escape the radiation. If our contact in Warlord Inferno's camp was correct about Lemur, the technoloner, being in these mountains, this would be the most likely spot for him to hide out. Keeping the installation in a state of abandonment would be a good ruse."

"So we're going then, right?" Whisper turned to Swash with the expectant expression of a child.

For Swash, leaving the rover meant he needed to trust someone else to be in charge, and that level of confidence didn't come easily. The lesson that life and death decisions should be handled by the captain had come at too high a price. And there always seemed to be some threat on the horizon. Checking on the old satellite station, however, wasn't something he could delegate. No matter what they saw up there, one thing remained constant. Danger. "You and I are going up there. Roach, I want you to remain at the helm."

"Going up where?" Stitch walked onto the bridge in full agroleathers.

"Nice of you to join us," Swash said. Though they'd shared bunks, her dogged determination to maintain her own space meant he had to ask each time he wanted alone time with her. The formality rankled.

Whisper pointed at the hologram. "Our boys found a satellite compound." Without Blade's emotionally distant presence, an informal familiarity had developed between the two couples. It was something Swash didn't approve of, but the women kept the jabs subtle enough that he found it hard to dole out his chastisement.

Stitch shook her head as she inspected the display. "Are you sure equally dividing our force is a good idea?"

One of the most annoying parts of being in a relationship with the medic, even if only partially, was her uncanny ability to parallel Swash's thoughts. "No one on board has a better feel for antennae than Whisper. I need to know if that thing is camouflaged to look abandoned or really is non-functional."

"That's not what I meant," Stitch said. "You've trained me on weapons. I can watch the Beast while the three of you check out the site."

He didn't want to delve back into the argument they'd been having regarding their weakened force since leaving Warlord Inferno's trading camp. "I'm not willing to leave anyone alone. If an enemy does spring on the Beast, it'll take someone running the observation drones while notifying me and another person on weapons."

"That's assuming someone shows up here," Stitch said. "It seems more likely that a platoon will come swarming out of the caves like angry death beetles."

Though she had a point, that didn't change his plan. "I'm the captain. All of our lives, including my own, are in my hands. Since we can't go rumbling up the mountain in the Beast without alerting any potential enemy, this is the best I can come up with. Whisper and I will use the sand flea. Blacked out and running on electrics the motorcycle will be less noticeable and lighter than the jump spider. If that lakebed is only a thin crust, the bike should be able to skirt over the hardpan. If it is Lemur up there, he's likely more interested in staying hidden than commanding a strike force."

"That's a big assumption," Stitch said.

"I've been working on that little two-wheeler, boss," Roach said. "It is in dirt-bike configuration, but it's still not as versatile as the sand rail."

Swash wondered if soliciting his crew's advice so often had resulted in each of them thinking they had a say in everything. "This time, I'll take stealth over versatility. Stitch is right about running into Lemur as being only one possibility. Scorch is still out there somewhere. The slippery little drill rig would just love to set up an ambush for us. If we're riding on one of his motorcycles, we might gain the benefit of the doubt if we stumble across his crew."

Stitch pointed at the edge of the display. "And once you get to the bottom of that ridge? Assuming you're right about there being people hiding up there, you'll be a prime target climbing the hill."

Swash had anticipated the question, though even he didn't like the answer he'd come up with. "We'll sneak in through the cave system."

Roach swung his head so quickly and so far that only a gen mod would have avoided a sprained muscle. "Boss, no. Those tunnels must be a labyrinth of intersections, dead ends, and cave-ins. You'd be lost as soon as you were out of sight of the entrance."

"I won't," Whisper said.

Swash turned his chair toward her, unwilling to ask the question that screamed in his head regarding the nature of her special skills and hearing.

Stitch put her hand on the girl's shoulder. "We've only begun scoping out your abilities. Your gen mod bat DNA is recessive. It's not like you've got sonar."

"That nurse you met in the hospital did," Whisper said.

Swash wasn't willing to invest their hopes on a fantasy. "She was a full mutation. You're not."

Whisper turned away from the hologram. "I'm telling you, Captain, I can do it. I know I can. Ever since I was a little girl, I've been comfortable in caves. I never once got lost in one."

Swash wasn't sure if he should ask how far those tunnels of her youth had extended. He probably didn't want to know. "I want a fallback plan in case Whisper's special skills aren't up to those of the cave dwellers we encounter."

Stitch crossed her arms under her breasts. "Other than leaving breadcrumbs along your path, I don't see what that would be."

"That's brilliant, Stitch" Roach said. "When I was in the tower saving Blade's sorry ass, we lined our communications buds up with one of Whisper's drones to make contact with Cypress. If Swash and Whisper take a case of those ear coms, they could leave one at each intersection. That way we could stay in contact."

Swash looked back at Stitch. "Would that satisfy you?"

"No." Her voice betrayed more frustration than logic. "But short of sending you in with a battalion, I don't know what would make me feel better."

Swash turned back to Whisper. "Daylight is still six hours away. That's more than enough time to make the crossing before we're spotted. You'd better return to your bunk and get what sleep you can. I doubt we'll be getting any once we head out."

Stitch put her hand on Swash's shoulder. "I prescribe the same for you. Roach can watch the Beast."

Swash turned to Roach. "Four hours, not a second longer."

❧

As Swash made himself comfortable on his mattress, Stitch put her hands on the ledge of the berth like she was about to climb up. "You're joining me?" He was never quite sure of her plans regarding their encounters.

"Don't be a fracking drill hole and scoot over. I prescribed you a nap, so you get me along with it to help you sleep."

Having her with him didn't always result in a restful sleep—at least not the times he relished. From her attitude, this wasn't going to be one of those liaisons. "What is with you, anyway? You've been moody for weeks."

After climbing in, she pulled down the rolling top to the berth. The fact that she hadn't shed her clothing couldn't mean anything good. "I'm scared."

He could come up with about a thousand reasons for her emotion, but he was pretty sure he would be wrong on every count. "You can talk to me about anything."

She favored him with a sheepish smile. "I don't know how to be in a romantic relationship. Okay? I thought I could overcome my past, but each time we're together physically my professional training kicks in."

In his experience, every woman was a bit distant during sex. He assumed that was just how females were wired. "Is that why you won't stay with me after sex? You can only allow yourself to be in my berth if it's for medicinal reasons?"

She lay on her side and snuggled her arm under her head as if trying to avoid any physical contact. "I suppose that's an accurate analysis."

"'Accurate analysis?' Good lord, I must be in trouble for you to sound so analytical while lying next to me."

She scrunched close enough to press her knee between his thighs. "You're not in trouble. If anything, you're my medicine." She stared up at him and frowned. "See? I'm doing it again."

"Is this about you growing up with a prostitute as a mother and a slave trader as a father?" He wasn't much good at figuring people out—especially women—but the parent-child dynamics had to have left their marks.

"Maybe, but that's only part of it. I don't have any problem with giving you my body, especially if I think you need the release. I worry about what you're doing as captain in charge of us all. I can tend to your wounds and use everything I have to keep you from illness. But in the end, all of those things are actions I would do for anyone on the Beast. Letting you *in*, and I mean really into my soul, isn't something I know how to do. I've never been in a relationship like this before. It scares me."

He took her hand from under her cheek. "Tell me how I can help. What do you need?"

Her sniffle could have either been a partial cry or a reaction to the cool, dry, recycled air. "For you to come back safe. I always worry when you, or anyone really, goes out on an away mission. But this is different somehow, and I don't know how to process what I'm feeling."

Swash wasn't any more experienced when it came to emotions than Stitch, and when it came to the physical nature of a relationship, she was a professional and him barely an amateur. "The trader at Inferno's camp referred to the guy lurking in these mountains as a technoloner. I've run into that type before. They don't have armies guarding the gates the way Whisper's mom did. Mostly, these recluses avoid people and keep their noses buried in books about the past. Sneaking through the tunnels is just a precaution to keep him from going into hiding like a mole retreating to his den. We'll be safe." By saying *we* instead of *me*, he hoped Stitch would feel more at ease with her emotions. It wasn't just him she was worried about, and that meant risking a lover was only a part of her fear.

With her hand still in his, she used her free hand to unfasten her top. "Don't lose hope in me. I want to make our relationship work, but it may take some time." She pulled his hand to between her breasts as if inviting him into her soul.

"Everyone's broken. There's no shame in trying to figure out where the damage lies. Any grouping of people is really just a mosaic of busted pieces."

2

---

*W*hisper couldn't sleep. Expecting her to lay quietly on her bunk while Swash and Stitch were likely getting it on and Roach was sitting all alone in the navigation chair was just fracked-up thinking. After giving the captain and medical officer enough time to get naked and focused on each other, Whisper pulled up the side of the metal drum. Even with her trained hearing, she couldn't detect the couple beneath red *Occupied* light. If they weren't getting it on, at least they weren't opening the berth. Years of sneaking, stealing, and spying had taught her how to move without being heard or seen. She climbed out of her berth and pulled the cover back down while only making the sounds normal to the rover sitting out in the open.

She couldn't remember going on an away mission with the captain, at least not one that involved any real degree of danger. Usually Blade had taken her out, and then there were the forever memorable and life-changing times Roach had escorted her off rover. She'd even spent some time with Stitch away from the others. But never Swash. As she crept onto the bridge, she wondered why that was. "Do you think the captain likes me?" she asked Roach while he was still focused on the holographic display of the mountain top.

He swiveled toward her. "What a strange question. Of course he likes you."

She leaned against the back wall of the bridge and crossed her arms. "Fine, trust then. Do you think he trusts me?"

He shrugged his cute little monkey shoulders. "Swash Jones doesn't trust anyone. That's how he stays alive."

"He trusts you." She couldn't believe that Roach could be so naive as to think the captain didn't put all of his faith in his second-in-command gen mod.

He got up and put his hands on her shoulders. "What's this all about?"

She hadn't realized how tight her muscles had become until he touched them. "What if we get up there and we don't find anything? The captain has already put you all in such danger because of my mission. Eventually, he's going to decide that enough is enough. He doesn't owe me anything—quite the opposite. If it weren't for the two of you, I'd still be a slave under Scorch."

Roach pulled her into his arms. The long, spindly, tendon limbs covered in short white-and-black hair gave her a sense of peace that she'd never found in anyone else's embrace. "The boss isn't the type to leave someone stranded. When he decides we need to go in a different direction, I guarantee you'll know the whys, wheres, and what-fors before he makes the change."

She snuggled her face to his chest. "And then I would have to leave the Beast. None of you have any idea how far my mother's influence extends. If we don't go after the satellites, she'll insist I leave you to continue with her plan."

He ran his long powerful fingers along her spine. "So that's it. You're afraid if we have one more failure the boss will lose interest and I'll have to decide whether I'm staying onboard the Beast or joining you on your fairy-tale quest."

She pulled her cheek from his tickling chest. "Would you?"

He looked up at the ceiling and sighed. "I'll do everything in my power to make sure I don't have to make that choice. I owe my past freedom to Swash, but I see my future happiness with you."

She snuggled back against him. "It wasn't fair of me to ask you that—especially since it's all theoretical. I'm just worried about coming up empty again."

He caressed her loose hair. "You should try to sleep."

"Only if you're holding me." She had slept in enough closets, corners, and cubbies to not be particular when it came to difficult positions. So long as she was in Roach's arms, she'd feel bathed in love and luxury no matter her body's contortion.

He took the navigation chair and held out his long arms to her. "I promise to have you up in plenty of time to convince the others that you slept in your bunk as instructed."

She tried to restrain her excitement, but she still felt like she was a kid bouncing into his lap.

WHISPER WOKE up in her bunk without knowing how she got there. She assumed Roach had carried her like he would a small sleeping child. The image made her curl up in the blanket. But when the thought transitioned to what a child based on their union might look like, her blood ran cold. The prophylactics Stitch had proscribed to both of them would prevent an unwanted pregnancy—and the horrific result of two gen mods of differing species—but the assurance didn't make her feel any better. Though they might achieve long-term committed status, they could never reproduce. *He'd be such a wonderful father.*

"Are you up?" Roach's voice over the intercom made her force back a tear.

She reached up and turned on the connection. "Yep. Thanks for carrying me to bed."

"You were sleeping so hard I didn't want to wake you. Swash will be up in a couple of minutes."

It was going to be a long day, and she had no idea when they'd return or even *if* they'd return. "I'm going to grab a shower." She turned off both the *Send* and *Receive* buttons on the intercom before Roach made some comment about joining her.

When she opened her berth, she found Stitch standing beside the hatch. "I'd like to give you a quick checkup before you head out."

Whisper eased out of her bunk. "Are you worried I'm going to contract some bat disease while I'm in the cave system?"

Stitch fidgeted against the metal wall as Whisper climbed out of her berth. "The thought crossed my mind. Trying to anticipate what mischief each of you is about to get into provides me with a lot of nightmare material."

The brightly lit medical bay smelled of disinfectant as Whisper took the patient's seat. "And what has your active imagination come up with for this trip?"

"Try harder not to get bit this time." Stitch took her usual chair and fumbled with her vials. "Your biology can fight off anything a rat can dose you with, but bats are another matter. Anything they're carrying would be hard for me to cure."

Even with all of the caves along the ridges where she'd grown up, Whisper had never seen a bat. It was as if they intentionally avoided her. With Stitch's history of studying gen mods, she hoped the woman might be able to answer some questions. "Will I be able to talk to them?"

Stitch stopped toying with the miniature glass jars. "I can't imagine that they'd be able to understand you, even if you could put out a sonar signal. I'm hoping you'll be able to hear them, though. Your hearing is beyond a normal human's ability."

The medic's testing since leaving Warlord Inferno's camp hadn't been unpleasant. Stitch had treated Whisper like they were two researchers bouncing ideas off each other then trying them out. Never once did she feel like the guinea pig she knew she was. "If I can't be understood by the bats, could I somehow scare them away? I'd rather not have a colony of them flapping about my head."

Stitch leaned back in her chair. "We're beyond my expertise in the matter. As recessive characteristics, what I found in the gen mods I studied was a wide range of abilities. I wish I were going with you."

Whisper had never heard Stitch request to go on a potentially dangerous mission. "I'll be fine with the captain."

Stitch looked at her notebook like there was some answer or threat on the pages that Whisper didn't know about. "Physically, I'm sure you will be. It's your mental health I'm worried about." She flipped the journal closed as if not wanting the pages to hear what she was about to say. "On Diablo Island, one of our tests was to lock a suspected gen mod in a cage with a member of their genetic donor species to see how they would interact."

Whisper couldn't imagine being locked in a cage with a bat. "What happened?"

Stitch turned away from her desk. "Even when normal people are put together with chimpanzees, there's a mutual recognition. We've never really been able to explain it, as it's more emotional than logical, but the two species gravitate toward identifying characteristics they have in common. If a chimp extends her finger or hand, a person will do likewise. For the gen mods, that connection is even stronger. I wouldn't go so far as to say it was like a woman's reaction to an infant, but there are similarities."

"So they might help me?" Whisper wasn't sure how any of this mattered in regard to finding the technoloner in the cave system.

"They might." Stitch didn't sound like she believed that would be the case. "For most gen mods, their reaction to being close to a member of their biological animal lineage stopped at fascination. For others, however, the meeting proved unsettling. And I mean that in the psychoanalytical sense."

"They lost their minds?" A cold chill ran through Whisper's heart.

"You have to understand, the test was designed to flush out actual gen mods. The close physical proximity, use of a cage, and forced interactions would make anyone a little jumpy." She took Whisper's hands. "If you can't scare off the colony and find yourself surrounded by flying bats, stay calm. Don't let their chirping, flapping, and high-pitched sonar make you forget who you are. And stay close to Swash."

"Are you seriously afraid that I'm going to wander off alone in a dark damp cave?"

Stitch smiled knowingly. "Don't play the innocent with me. Roach told me about you trying to sneak off when you two were checking out the trading store."

"That was different." Whisper made a mental note to hammer Roach on his lack of confidentiality. "I knew Roach was right there. Those shopkeepers weren't really a threat, even if they thought they were. I've been in much rougher situations."

"I know you have, but this isn't like the other threats you've encountered. You can't sneak away from your own thoughts. The gen mods who succumbed to their darkness said the thought just kept circling around them like a noose getting tighter with each rotation."

Whisper wasn't sure she wanted to know, but she had to ask. "What thought?"

Stitch stared at their clasped hands. "That they had more in common with the animal in front of them than the humans outside the cage conducting the tests."

3

It wasn't a lack of faith in Roach's ability to watch over the Beast that nagged at Swash as he got the motorcycle out of the engine bay. Without Blade, they were shorthanded. The problem of too many people to protect and not enough expertise in combat had been why Swash had taken on the hired gun in the first place. And after having him available during crises, the lack of the warrior was even more noticeable.

With the motorcycle out of the way, Swash inspected the wall containing the Beast's arsenal. The plasma cannons would only work with the rover's power supply, but that didn't mean they could be left in storage. He lifted them individually from their racks and set them on the floor to be loaded into the mounts on the catwalk. If things turned ugly, Roach and Stitch wouldn't have time to get the heavy and cumbersome primary weapons ready. The board loaded with blasters looked like an old man's display of well-organized tools. Each had worn handles, scorch marks on the barrels, and random dents from being used as hand weapons of last resort. Swash picked two of the smaller guns for Whisper and stashed his usual high-capacity weapons in the holsters at his legs. He considered grabbing a couple for Roach and Stitch, but they weren't leaving the rover. They could pick their own favorites.

It was hauling the non-lethal components that rankled him. The supply of earbuds made sense. Using them like breadcrumbs would mean they could talk to the Beast, and that at least meant Swash would be alerted if something went wrong. Food and water were necessary evils in his opinion. As a boy, he'd been taught how to scavenge what he needed while off rover. Carrying too much stuff not only weighed him down, it also contained hints about where he'd come from. Anything that led back to the Beast posed a threat to the rest of the crew.

He grabbed the climbing rope and grappling hook. No matter how far the caves extended into the mountain, the climb wasn't likely to be an easy one. If they were lucky, they'd encounter an air shaft.

He hefted the rope and backpack. *Luck* was the problem that made the hairs on the back of his neck stand on end and irritated the hell out of his nerve endings. If he were heading out with Roach or Blade, he could rely on their expertise. Conducting a maneuver with Stitch meant the woman would be constantly on guard for any incoming threats—even if they were often mostly imagined. Whisper, however, seemed to be attracted to danger like a moth to a flame—or more appropriately like a bat to some unknown sonar signal. She was good at what she knew, but she was unpredictable.

"Boss, Whisper's just about ready," Roach said over the com.

He would have liked to pick his first officer's brain about Whisper, but as her boyfriend, Roach wasn't exactly impartial. "As the last one to go climbing, other than the rope and tackle what would you suggest I take with us?"

"As little as possible. Every ounce feels like ten pounds after hours of hanging onto a rope. I'll come back and give you a hand with the motorcycle."

Swash wondered if the women had also picked up Roach's conspiratorial tone over the com link. He wanted to talk in private, not that it was a surprise. They met in the crew quarters. Together they lifted the bike out of the side hatch then closed the door behind them. With a solid wall of metal between them and the women, Swash removed his earbud. "What's up?"

Roach attached the hoist hooks to the front and back of the motorcycle. "We can't afford to lose another crew member."

Any mission included the possibility of death. "I'll do my best."

Roach lowered the bike to the ground. "You always do, but that's not what I meant. Whisper's worried that one more failure and you'll pull the plug on helping her mother. If you do, she may have to leave the Beast."

Swash checked the bag and rope over his shoulders then descended the ladder. "And here I thought you were worried one of us was going to get killed. Don't worry so much." He hoped his nonchalant manner would put the kid off articulating what Swash already knew. If Whisper left, Roach would be right behind her. A two-person crew for the Beast would mean certain death at their next ambush. And though Roach and Whisper had their unique skills, they likely wouldn't even last as long as Swash and Stitch if left on their own.

WITH WHISPER on the back of the bike and him at the controls, Swash felt like he should impart some words of wisdom to Roach and Stitch or at least leave orders not to get killed. He couldn't come up with anything that didn't sound foolish. "Don't do anything I wouldn't do." He hit the throttle before either of them could respond.

Whisper hung onto the seat's side rails as Swash ran along the old beach. "How far do you think we can get using the motorcycle?"

As much to shut her up as to make her hold on better, he aimed the motorcycle straight down into the dried lake bottom. She got the hint. Her hands shot from the rails to his sides, and her body snuggled against his. The only way to maneuver a dirt bike with a passenger was for the two body weights to act as one. "I'll get us to the entrance of the mine, but it's going to be a bumpy ride. It helps if you hang on tight and don't watch where we're going. Just let your body mimic my movements."

"Yes, Captain."

During his lifetime on the Beast, Swash had been

instructed on how to drive all manner of vehicles. As a kid, motorcycles had been one of his favorites. He swung the silent two-wheeler side to side against the ground to determine the earth's solidity. As an area that had once been filled with water, there was no way of knowing how solid the ground was a couple of inches under the dried and hard-packed silt. As the rear wheel sliced through ground, it tossed up dark chunks along with the tan dirt. He got the bike back under him and kept their weight evenly distributed to avoid slipping on the differing substrates.

"Was that necessary?" Whisper asked from against his back.

"Always know what's underneath you in case you're attacked. It's important to identify strengths and weaknesses early. Those were some of my grandfather's first combat lessons."

Her hands pulled tightly against his stomach. "And what's your assessment of me?"

Facing danger wasn't the time for self-doubt, but it also wasn't the time to blow smoke up someone's ass. "You're a fair aim with a blaster. Had your life taken different turns, you would have made a decent assassin, but not because of your weapon skills. You shoot with cold precision. That determination counts more in battle than a steady hand. Your biggest challenge is knowing who to shoot. In a firefight it's not always easy to tell friend from foe."

"I would never shoot you or any of the others."

He didn't doubt her. "That's not what I meant. Your comrades are one thing; identifying strangers who are on your side is another."

"Do you think we'll be in that kind of a fight?" she asked.

He had no idea what they'd be facing. He liked to keep his mind open to whatever came at them instead of getting stuck in some preconceived impression of their enemy. "I think we need to be ready for anything. Now settle in back there and let me drive this thing. We should be at the cave entrance in about half an hour."

4

*S*wash stashed the blacked-out bike behind the collapsed guard station that nestled against the side of the canyon leading to the cave. The spot was far enough from the entrance that anyone leaving the hole in the cliff wouldn't immediately notice it, but close enough that he and Whisper could jump on the bike and shoot down the mountain without interference if they ended up being pursued. "Okay, Whisper. You're the self-professed expert on caves. That makes you the leader."

He'd seen her in action enough times on the Beast and gotten enough reports from the previous away missions to know about her game face. The playful, damaged, and almost innocent persona transitioned into a stealthy, focused, and dangerous weapon as easily as she pulled her hood over her head. "The technoloner won't be in this lower section of caves," she said. "He'll be above the satellite installation where he can command a view of the whole valley."

"Guards?" Swash asked as much to watch her analytical skills as to get her opinion.

"If there are any, it would make sense to have them in this lower labyrinth. As the bottom section of the mine, we'll be walking into a maze of tunnels, dead ends, and who knows what else. If it were me, that's where I'd station my security, but I'd keep them hidden until my prey got lost in the dark. Then they could easily keep the intruders trapped without the need to engage. Someone approaching the installation would either need to climb the cliff and risk being seen, or do what we're about to do by going through the mountain. Either way, it wouldn't take a large force to control the area."

That was pretty much his assessment as well. He pulled his pack off his shoulder and removed one of the communication buds. "We're going in," he said into it before wedging the small earpiece into a split in the overhead beam.

Whisper snuck through the boarded-up opening as quietly as the wind blowing between the slats. Swash wasn't able to be quite as stealthy, but he doubted there would be anyone standing guard at the door. And if they were, as Whisper said, they likely wouldn't bother engaging in battle if they didn't feel they had to.

Inside the dark tunnel he scanned the shadows for any sign of Whisper. "Where are you?" Though he kept his voice low, he feared the sound might reverberate down the shaft.

Her hand snuck into his as if a piece of the wall had just

come to life. She didn't say anything as she crept ahead of him into the dark. After a few hundred feet and a couple of bends in the tunnel, he was completely lost, but his eyesight had adjusted to the low-light conditions.

She squeezed his hand once and pointed to a ledge that projected out from an intersection of shafts.

He snatched another earbud and did his best to line it up with where they'd come in. He had to keep his head ducked down as she led him along the next passage. All he could do was hope she had some inclination of where she was going, though he couldn't imagine how she'd be any better at navigating the confusing switchbacks, inclines, and intersections than he could. Letting someone else take the lead never came naturally for him, and he was beginning to think this whole subterranean hike had been one big lethal mistake. He was just about to say so when she stopped abruptly and held up her hand.

"Bats." She mouthed more than spoke the word.

Stitch had warned him that Whisper would be susceptible to anything the flying rodents might be carrying.

She leaned in so close to his ear that he could feel her breath. "They're not alone."

A high-pitched whistle that Swash felt more than heard deep in his ears had him covering them from the internal pain. At the sound of thousands of flapping wings, he ignored the piercing tone, grabbed his cape, and threw his body over Whisper, pinning her to the wall. Small furry bodies struck his back like an avalanche of rats. Their acrid odor made him close his eyes as if that would somehow shut his nose as well. With each impact, the furry flying fiends screeched and bit at the cloak, but the Kevlar layer prevented their teeth from breaking through.

"I'm one of you, and we're not here to fight," Whisper yelled.

The bats disappeared down a side corridor as fast as they'd attacked. "You're a batling?" The question echoed down from high up in the cave.

Whisper pushed against Swash, but he wasn't sure he should let her go. "It's okay, Captain. I have a protective cape too you know."

Reluctantly, he backed away. "If you hear flapping, duck."

She moved into the center of the passage, much to his distress. Safety lay against the wall, not out in the open. Standing with her feet spread and her hands on the hips of her leathers, she looked far more invincible than Swash thought justified given their position. "I'm Whisper Payne. I come from the southern range. I want to talk to the person who operates the satellite compound."

The chuckle from deep in the tunnel made Swash tense for battle. "You sound like a child who's wandered into a research library and only wants to look at the comic books. I have far more to offer you than connecting a technological wire to those floating tin cans in space."

Swash considered grabbing Whisper's hand and running back the way they'd come—if he only knew which way that was. Losing her to the shadowy bat creature would result in Roach demanding they conduct a rescue. Swash leaned out from the wall toward her. "We're only here for your mission."

"Maybe this is my mission," she said loud enough for anyone to hear. "And even with our blasters, I strongly doubt we'd be able to fight our way out of here. What harm is there in hearing what he has to say?"

Swash could come up with a lot of potentially devastating consequences, but he wasn't in a position to argue with her. He adjusted his earbud, hoping for a little support from the home troops. "Roach, have you got me?"

All he heard in response was static.

"Your friend can't hear you." The masculine voice boomed down the tunnel.

Swash stepped away from the wall. He and Whisper were on their own against an unknown force who could command the bats that threatened from every tunnel. "What do you want?" he asked.

"My name is Aural. Whisper Payne is a name I've heard before. She has a right to know about her heritage. Listen to what I have to say, and I'll give you passage through my caves to meet with Lemur. Or if you prefer, you can turn around and follow my bats back to your motorcycle."

Whisper turned to Swash with the same enthusiasm she showed when she'd found some music device that would take up far too much room in the Beast. "This is important to me, Captain."

Swash hated being out of touch with the Beast, but turning around and leaving her there with the cave dweller wasn't an option. "Please make it fast, Whisper. Roach and Stitch aren't equipped to deal with problems. The longer we're away and they're stationary in the Beast, the more likely something's going to go wrong."

5

Whisper couldn't stop staring at the man, or batling as he called his kind. The short black bristly hair on his head and the tips of his pointy ears showed signs of gray. His sharp windswept features looked like he was ready for flight, though he lacked the wings to do so. The black cape he wore dusted the ground as he paced in front of his wall of books. "Does every batling have a fascination with books?" she asked.

He looked at the wall like he'd never noticed them. "I suppose when someone is born different, they seek to find out why."

"And what have you found?" Swash asked.

Aural kept his hands behind his back as he turned toward Swash. "That we weren't accidents or freaks from some mad scientist." He spread his arms. "What you see before you is the result of extensive bioengineering and careful breeding."

Whisper wasn't sure she wanted to hear the batling's truth, but if he was going to offer an alternative to Roach and Stitch's story, he was going to have to back it up. "I heard the gen mods were the result of experiments by rogue scientists."

He nodded at her. "That's the fiction the powers that be used on the outside world as their basis for rounding up our kind. If you think about it though, the explanation doesn't make much sense. Scientists all over the country independently mess around with discarded DNA samples and end up with monsters? It's just not even a good story."

Swash leaned against the rock wall. "Then what is the truth?"

Aural waved at his wall of books. "Novels from the twenty-first century are full of plot lines regarding genetic manipulation. In spite of what people might have believed at the time, government scientists read those stories as more than something to pass the time. Some of their best ideas came from those fiction writers—as well as the dangers to look out for. Gen mods were created by the military, not a disconnected group of mad scientists out to save the world." He nodded at Whisper. "You and I are the result of their attempt to bypass the broken communications network."

Whisper shook her head. "That doesn't make any sense. My mission is part of an attempt to fix the network, not replace it with gen mods."

"Missions change." He motioned toward the door back into the cave. "Come with me. Let me show you something."

Unlike the tunnels they'd scampered through, Aural's

rock walls were smooth, clean, and dry. Stairs were carved into the basalt ground. At the top of the volcanic vent, they emerged into what appeared to be a naturally formed chamber with human-size blast holes in the walls. "What is this place?" Whisper asked.

"This is how we communicate," Aural said. He turned toward one of the openings. "If I send out a sonar signal in this direction, my voice will be heard all the way into the Canadas." He pointed in the opposite direction. "That way and I'll be heard as far south as the nuclear trench."

Whisper leaned against one of the pillars next to a hole. "How?"

"There are repeater towers like this one that direct and reinforce my sonar. This network extends all along the tops of the Rocky Mountains and down the slopes as far as our sonar can reach without enhancement. The military had grand plans of sidestepping the communication satellite system when they built this network but not the time to extend it beyond this mountain range. Using us as sentries, they not only had a secure communications network along the ridge that separated the eastern and western alliances, they also had the ability to use us to detect incursions by way of our sonar. And with our bat emissaries, we could keep an eye on everything that happened in these mountains. Most of these stations are abandoned now. There are less than a handful of batlings that still maintain the network."

"What does any of this have to do with me?" Whisper had always feared that one day she'd be shown that her life had no meaning, and apparently this was that day.

"We're familiar with Brigadier General Payne. Your mother intentionally bred with one of my kind. We believe she needed a spy and felt the only way to get one she could truly trust was to create one herself. If we're correct, this hopscotch mission she has you on has less to do with those old satellite dishes and more to do with rooting out our batling brothers and sisters. Though that's mostly conjecture on my part."

"How?" Whisper asked. "I didn't even know you existed until a few months ago."

"She intentionally kept you in the dark. Each satellite dish you've been investigating was built as high on the mountain range as possible so it could watch the most amount of sky."

Swash nodded. "Just like this sonic volcanic room. So you're saying that where there's a listening station, there's also a sonic relay? But what interest would Sky Payne have regarding your kind? From what Whisper has told me, she's on a mission not sanctioned by the military, so it would have to be personal for her."

"Put it down to competing programs, or maybe sour synth-grapes that she wasn't included in either program to begin with. She might even be looking to bypass her own military commanders by trying to solicit our help."

Swash had the furrowed brow Whisper had seen before when the captain was working on an especially vexing issue. "Assume for a moment that she is on the outside of both programs. I can see how she'd know about the satellites. They aren't exactly a secret. But your batling network is a different story. Why would she go to all of the trouble of birthing a bat gen mod without a solid understanding of what she was up against? The information would need to be fairly well distributed among the military."

Aural shook his head. "The books and manuals in my library aren't the type of references a person would find on a typical military base. They came from secret medical labs that had been looted after the wars. You look to me to be enough of a warrior to know that secret missions have a way of being kept hidden even from those in charge. The gen mod development program was able to hide its existence by keeping those who knew about it down to a minimum. As for Sky Payne, we can watch her actions but not read her intentions. Who knows? She might even have actually fallen in love with Whisper's father and he told her of our presence. Our fear is that she may be trying to gain military favor by destroying all evidence of the breeding program, including us. And without us, the satellites become all the more vital."

Swash bit his lip. "I think you might be getting a little carried away with your own mythology. All you can do is talk among yourselves, admittedly over a vast distance, but nowhere near what a satellite system could achieve. And as you said yourself, there aren't many of you left. I don't see the threat you'd pose to the military. It's not like you're stockpiling weapons to finish the self-extinction that mankind has already begun. Why wouldn't they choose to just leave well enough alone?" He leaned out one of the blow-holes. "If you could live in peace, it seems to me that both sides would still have a lot to offer each other."

"The military doesn't want to be blamed for our existence," Aural said. "But as to your suggestion that we could work together, it comes down to a question of who's in control. As you can see, we don't require the government's technology to conduct our communication." He tapped on the volcanic rock wall. "Even if they were to bomb these repeating rooms, we could still send out our sonic signals. They have nothing to hold over us, and that scares them."

"And what are you holding over them?" Swash asked. "The wars ended when I was just a kid. Even as a secret unit, if the military were worried about you being discovered, why didn't they bomb you back then? Truces only hold if the stronger party has something to lose."

"We control the mountains, and the military elite knew it. Now what's left of those little military bases are like small, well-armed boats on the vast ocean. And if you'll forgive the mixed-gen mod metaphor, we're the sharks patrolling the waters. But sharks only have power so long as the hunter doesn't know where they are. Since remnants of the military continue to exist, we have to believe some aspect of the secret gen mod development program does as well. Once the secret unit can track our movements, they can focus their attack and clean up the mess they left behind. To prevent an all-out original versus gen mod war, they will only conduct their final extermination once they have all of our locations, which is one of the reasons many of my kin remain on the move." He turned toward Whisper. "And our fear is that's why Sky Payne created you. By connecting the satellites while discovering our locations, she'll be in a prime bargaining position with the elite powers."

Whisper shook her head. "That's not true. That can't be true. My mother is trying to save what's left of humanity."

"On that last count we agree, but where you believe she's doing that in an attempt at restarting an ancient technology, in reality she may be doing it by limiting the growth of our species. Batlings and the other gen mods are the logical next evolution of what was known as humanity. Homo Sapiens are on their way toward extinction—out evolved by their own creation—but they're not going to go quietly. That's why a generation ago the story of mutant monsters was put out into the public neurosis. The government hoped the general population of originals would control what they couldn't—at least not without exposing their own part in our development."

"So I'm just some homing pigeon designed to seek you out so my mother can exterminate you? If that's so, why didn't you just kill me as soon as I revealed my identity?"

He smiled at her. "Your mother doesn't have the reach she thinks she does. And unlike humans, we batlings still value life."

Whisper knew a con job when she heard one. "I'm not buying it. Since you didn't kill me, I must have some value to you. What do you want from me?"

Aural faced her. "Deception. Continue with your mother's quest, but don't say anything about us. Sky Payne is a patient woman. I doubt she'll ever directly ask if you've seen anything out of the ordinary. She doesn't really have to. I'm certain your reports to her detail anyone you find, whether they're running the installation or not. From here on, any satellite station you happen upon, you'll tell her was abandoned long ago."

Swash paced the small alcove. "Up until today, that hasn't been a lie."

Whisper stood with the same determined stance she'd had in the tunnel. "I still don't see how this is any better for you than killing me. You're hiding something."

Aural crossed his arms and smiled. "You're a very bright batling, Whisper Payne. So long as your mother receives your reports, she'll stay tucked away in that camp up on her mountain peak. Ask yourself, what would happen if you had died in one of those slave camps you grew up in or out here in the wilds with that rover next to you? Your life has been in constant peril, and your mother, as a military commander, would know that. What would you do in her position?"

Whisper wanted to scream, but the sound of frustration stuck in her throat. "I'd have someone else trained and ready to take my position. Someone she was equally as sure of."

Swash moved in close to Whisper's side. "Do you mean Shadow?"

Whisper turned to Aural. "She's my sister, isn't she?"

The batling shrugged. "See it from your mother's perspective. When you've created one good warrior, why not repeat the process? Honestly, we don't know how many children Sky Payne has produced. Clearly, she hasn't had any since taking on her current posting. She's played the long game by only having children when she could do so without the pregnancies being noticed."

Whisper thought back on her childhood. "She couldn't have had very many. She sold me off at nine years old, and I would have remembered if she'd been pregnant at the time."

"That's helpful," Aural said. "Your mother has been up on that mountain top for five years, leaving fourteen unaccounted for. We do believe Shadow is your sister. Her age matches up with the time you left. The pregnancy might have even been the reason Sky sent you out into the world. Though watching Sky Payne for any sign of maternal affection toward the waif is like watching a rock while waiting for it to move."

Whisper wasn't sure she was ready for more revelations, but she didn't know if she'd get another opportunity. "What about the monkey-based gen mods?" She felt guilty for asking. Potentially knowing more about Roach than he knew about himself seemed like a betrayal, but on the other hand, he might want the information.

"Consider the late twenty-first century," Aural said. "Humanity's wars were brute-force affairs. Spies, snipers, and special forces were the elite. To be one of them required skills and training beyond what most people could achieve."

Swash leaned against a column. "Skills a monkey hybrid would have as natural parts of their DNA."

"They call themselves monklings. They can scale buildings and squeeze into places where an original would get stuck and die. Originals think of gen mods as monsters without the mental capacity they'd attribute to a dog. The truth is we were created because humans are the brutes."

"Are there any others?" Whisper asked.

"Of the original gen mod species? Not that we know of. The program was one of the last conducted by the unified government's military. When the communication system finally did fall completely, a domino effect took place. Those in charge had enough time to destroy much of the evidence. Had they been caught creating genetically superior species, they would have been the first condemned by the general population."

"What about the offspring of batlings and monklings?" Swash asked.

"We call them the spawn. Obviously, monkeys and bats don't breed naturally. The spawn are the outcome of man's arrogance. The genetic wheel of chance is spun with each new birth. Other than that, I know very little about them. The research material I rely on was recorded before the central government fell, and the spawn are a relatively recent development."

"You seem to know quite a lot," Whisper said.

"This ridge line was the last bastion for the old government. Brigadier General Payne may be loyal to a splinter militia, but before the fall, her garrison was a part of the original army. Those in charge never really destroy all information, no matter what they say to their superiors."

Whisper didn't think she could take any more information about her heritage. "If we're going to fool my mother, I'm going to need something usable regarding the key master. We've come up empty too many times. You said information was left behind. Have you run across anything about the satellites?"

"My interests have been in saving what information I can find regarding the gen mod program. I haven't been overly concerned with what happened to the failed space technology." He nearly spit out the words as if the very thought of the space birds revolted him.

"You've been very informative," Swash said. "But as Whisper said, we need to find out what's happening with that old satellite station and contact Brigadier General Payne's warbird if you have any hope of staying under her radar."

Aural motioned toward a peak along the ridge. "You'll find Lemur up there."

6

---

*W*hisper had the utmost respect for the captain, but he really didn't know much about gen mods. She could tell from the way he stood stone cold on the ridge line staring out toward the Beast miles away that he resented the delay caused by meeting Aural. But if she had turned down the mysterious ruler of the labyrinth, they likely wouldn't have ever made it out of the tunnels. A little whistle from the batling here, or unaccounted for light there, and she could have mistakenly led Swash right into the center of the mountain instead of discovering a way out. Besides, someone so knowledgeable regarding her heritage wasn't the type of person she was likely to find again. She looked up into the night sky. "I guess we were down there longer than I thought."

Swash roused himself from his contemplation then secured the final earbud to a tree trunk in line with both the cave system and the drone hovering high over the Beast. He activated his com link. "Roach, have you got me?"

She turned on hers as well while hoping Swash wouldn't go blabbing about her agreeing to talk to the human bat. Maybe the conversation would be kept short enough for her to maintain her focus on their mission.

"It's good to hear your voice, boss. You gave us both a bit of a scare being silent for so long. I guess it was harder getting out of those tunnels than we imagined. All's quiet on the home front." Hearing Roach's voice put a lump in her throat.

"We ran into a situation that couldn't be avoided," Swash said. "We'll fill you in later. How does our position look from down there?"

"A colony of bats blasted out of a hole near the top of the ridge. Looked like a flapping volcanic eruption. Stitch wants to know if you two had anything to do with the exodus."

"How's Whisper," Stitch asked in the very precise tone she used when frustrated.

"I'm fine." Whisper tried to employ the same precision of suppressed annoyance.

"The furry beasts made an attack on us," Swash said. "But the Kevlar cloaks warded them off. No bites and no life-threatening vectors in either of us—at least not that we're aware of. And with the breadcrumb communication link connected both at the base and top of the cave system, we should be able to work our way back down and out of here once we're done with the technoloner."

She wasn't sure if leaving out the conversation with Aural had been his way of keeping Roach calm or if it was an unspoken hint to her that their communication link might be compromised. Either way, she didn't see any point in adding to the captain's narrative.

"Whisper," Stitch said, "it will be the middle of the night by the time you make it to the installation. Will that make any difference in you finding out what this guy is up to?"

People had such odd ways of interpreting what they saw in the sky. Being dark out, the satellites showed up as bright dots, some of them moving too slowly and precisely for any shooting star and others completely stationary relative to the rotating universe behind them. But being visible at night, the human assumption was that somehow they were easier to find and contact than during the day. "In terms of contacting a space bird, it shouldn't matter."

"And if the Lemur has special abilities?" Though innocent enough, Roach's question made her eyes burn.

He doesn't know about the guy in the tunnel, and I did suspect Lemur of being one of us. She focused on what she knew. "I originally jumped to a conclusion that is looking more and more to be false."

"Okay," Roach said with a tinge of suspicion in his voice. "But names have meaning. If he's going by the label of a nocturnal animal, that might mean he's more comfortable in the dark. You spent the day in the caves where he couldn't see you. Tonight, in spite of the dark, you could be walking straight into a trap."

She squeezed her eyes closed in frustration at herself. Not every self-proclaimed title referenced gen mod enhancements, but some did. "You're right. We'll be careful."

~

Swash hunched down on the dark side of a gray boulder and pulled his black cape over his head. He kept a hand on Whisper's back to prevent her from edging out too far where she could be seen. The climb had taken most of the night, sapping what little energy they had after the journey through the tunnel system. Their food and water had been depleted. Hunger and fatigue were bad influencers when it came to dangerous decisions.

The light from the window of the metal and wood cabin that perched on a rock ledge overlooking the satellite dish didn't ease Swash's apprehension. Whisper had already heard more information than she could process for one day. Having to finally confront one of her mother's mysterious key holders might overload the poor girl's brain. With the climb through the caves, meeting with Aural, and the final ascent along the ridge, it had already been a long twenty-four hours. "I can go alone if you want. All we need to do is have him ping your mother's satellite."

She looked at him like he'd lost his mind. "And if this Lemur character is actually the key master? No. I'm going in, and don't even think of stopping me."

Exhaustion had a way of fraying on nerves, and Swash didn't want to make a tense situation worse. "Wouldn't dream of it." He snuck past a termite-infested tree, wiping the ugly buggers from his cape. "I suppose there's no point in sneaking up on him."

The door opened as he crossed beyond the line of rotting timber. "You two must be the fools who stumbled into Aural's pits. Come on in. I've got some tea brewing. You must be tired."

Swash had trouble remembering his last instance of easy social interaction. Typically, he had to wrestle an enemy to the ground then force the information he needed out of them—or he was the one sitting in the interrogation chair. He stepped into the shack before Whisper had a chance to do something foolish like trigger whatever trap Lemur might have in place.

The single room looked like something Whisper would have designed. One entire wall was made up of technological boxes that did god-knows what. Display screens, dials, readouts—both digital and analog—were all jumbled together like they'd been tossed into a heap while still active. At the back corner opposite the humming boxes, Lemur pulled a pot off a wood-burning stove. Furniture, if the collection of sticks and cushions could be called that, crowded the space from the front door to the makeshift kitchen. Whatever passed for a bathroom must have been outside of the cabin.

Lemur set the three mugs on a flat surface that must have served as his table. Though Swash wasn't well versed in the social niceties, some actions were second nature, like letting the guest choose their cup. He took the one closest while Whisper picked the far one. Lemur picked up the remaining mug and took a deep swig.

Seeing that the man didn't instantly die, Swash took a tentative sip. The stuff tasted like liquid compost. "We won't take up much of your time. A junk dealer in Warlord Inferno's trading camp said you often bring in old technology. We're interested in what you do with your stash and, more specifically, why you're camped out next to an old satellite dish."

Lemur settled into the lone lounge chair. The thing seemed to close in around him. "Let's cut out the reconstituted shit. Aural already told me what you two are up to."

Whisper bent her butt down to a fabric-covered heap of junk. Sitting wasn't the word Swash would use for the action, but it did put her on Lemur's eye level. "We weren't sure if you two got along."

"Look, my batling friend has his form of survival, and I've got mine. As the only two sentient beings up here, it was inevitable that we would have some interactions. I suppose if you're the last two people on a desert island, even if you've been on opposite sides at one time, you find interests in common to keep you going."

"And what is your answer?" Swash remained standing. The sooner Whisper was convinced this guy was just some nerdy loner and they got him to push his fancy button to notify General Payne the sooner they could start working their way back to the Beast.

"That's a tough one. I suppose when I first started listening to the sky I had hoped there was an answer up there—some lost piece of wisdom from our ancestors that would be the key to unlocking a solution to survival down here. I guess that sounds pretty naive at this point."

Anything that didn't lead to putting food in the belly or repelling attacking raiders qualified as naive in Swash's view of life. "So you didn't find some technological version of the lost library of Alexandria?"

Lemur took a drink of his concoction as if it were alcoholic and he needed the fortification. "What I found was a space war. There are satellites up there armed with weapons that would be unimaginable on Earth. Apparently, once the military engineers took human life out of the equation, they decided nuclear weapons, high-powered lasers, and anything else that could wreak whole-scale destruction became fair game. The communication network wasn't just shut off, it was blasted to bits."

"Then what's the point in sitting up here diddling your antennae?" Whisper asked.

Lemur shrugged. "I stopped looking for the needle in the space haystack long ago, but that doesn't mean there isn't a computer data bank somewhere down here on Earth with the answers I seek. And if there is, the satellites might be the only way to access it. If I leave my bird on for too long though, those ex-military robots would be able to zero in on my location, and not just that of my satellite, but this hilltop as well. Those space weapons weren't just armed to kill their own kind."

Swash chose his words carefully so he could be certain of the answer. "You mean to say they can shoot a spot on Earth from orbit with lasers or nuclear ordinance?"

"Before the satellite system went dark, that was one of the ways war was conducted," Lemur said. "What those birds are capable of now is anyone's guess. It's not like their nuclear missiles can be replaced once launched. I don't even know if they're being controlled from Earth or are on some form of attack autopilot. One of the reasons I keep diddling my antennae, as Whisper called it, is to prevent anyone from hacking one of those warbirds. I've seen them let loose a blast of lightning that stretched from one horizon to the other."

Whisper fidgeted in her seat. "Do you know about Brigadier General Sky Payne?"

"Your mother? Yeah, I know her. Aural keeps me informed about anyone who poses a threat to either of us. I wouldn't be at all surprised to discover that those warbirds are under her control."

"Between your story and Aural's," Swash said, "Sky Payne could be using Whisper as her personal targeting device."

"What about the key master?" Whisper asked questions like she was ripping off bandages, looking for the one that would reveal a still-lethal wound.

"You mean the head of some stealthy secret organization stealing satellites so he can build his communication network? Sounds to me like someone's been reading too many twenty-first century corporate thriller novels."

"So you don't believe this person exists?" Swash wondered if this might be the first really good news he'd found all day. If there was no key master, there was no need to keep hunting—at least not for the reason Sky Payne had set down. A reasonable story could be created to extricate Whisper from her mission.

Lemur refreshed his cup from the pot on the stove. "I'm more concerned about the rogue warbirds than I am with some nerd-led organization trying to break my code. Like all key holders, my computer gets hit with cyberattacks on a regular basis. Where they come from is anyone's guess— other satellites, antique ground-based telecommunication vehicles, hell I even had some guy try to crash a hack-drone into my dish. But I've never had someone try to access my bird in a way that I couldn't see coming a mile away. If any of the attempts was by the key master, he's not as skilled as your mother fears."

"Just because you haven't been successfully hacked, that doesn't mean he doesn't exist." Whisper sounded a lot like her mother.

"That's true," Lemur responded. He got up again and walked over to his bank of dials, gauges, and computer screens. With tea in hand, he started firing up the technology. When the screens displayed scrolling numbers he backed away. "All I can tell you is that I am not the key master. If you don't believe me, see for yourself."

Whisper struggled up from the sagging cushion. "There's only one thing my mother will accept, and that's if I ping her satellite from yours."

Lemur shrugged. "I suppose it's time I moved mine to a new orbit anyway. Do what you came here to do."

The way Whisper faced the controls reminded Swash of the first time he'd handled the Beast. "All of this for just one satellite?" she asked.

"I snag what I can from the outpost. Like Aural and his journals, I have to sift through a lot of garbage to find the gems."

7

The late morning sunlight tinged the bands of chemical-laced dust clouds a noxious orange as Swash pulled the motorcycle from its hiding spot at the base of the tunnel system.

"I'm still not getting anything from Roach or Stitch." Whisper had been calm enough while working through the caves. Out in the open, however, Swash's feeble hypothesis that Aural had shorted out the trail of breadcrumb earbuds with his sonic screech was wearing thin.

He needed to keep her from spiraling down the vortex of fear. "Stitch isn't half the drone pilot that you are. She probably fell asleep at the switch and our long-range hawk got stuck in a tree." All he could do was hope the answer was that simple.

The look Whisper gave him made it clear she didn't think his explanation made sense. "I know for a fact that

Roach would never drift off while I was away. Stitch wouldn't either when it came to you facing danger. Something's wrong. I can feel it."

Swash hopped on the electric motorcycle. "Only one way to find out. The sooner we get to them the sooner we can face the next challenge."

With Whisper on the back, Swash slalomed the bike down the hillside, dislodging rocks and dirt into an avalanche that kept pace with the rolling tires. He was way too far past the thirty hours of consciousness that Stitch had set as his maximum time awake if he hoped to maintain his strength and sanity. His eyes burned from the dust and tiredness. His arms and legs ached from the climb through the tunnel system and along the ridge. His heart beat hard from worry regarding the Beast and half of his crew. His head pounded like a jackhammer against the rock-pile of information he'd absorbed. At a smooth spot in their descent, he tapped his earbud to talk to Whisper over the cacophony of mountain and thoughts. "How are you holding up?"

"I honestly don't think I can take one more catastrophe."

At the remembered boulder, he swung the bike hard to the right and away from the falling rocks. "Just hang on. We'll be home before you know it."

She snugged her body to his and pulled hard against his stomach. With her face hidden against his back, he guessed she didn't want to see what had become of the Beast. He slid the wheels along the ruts he'd carved in the lake bed on the way to the caves.

"Shit." He yanked hard at the brakes, bringing the motorcycle to a stop at the upper lip of the ravine.

"What is it?" Whisper kept her face against his cloak.

"The Beast isn't here." From the smell of freshly burned wood, countless tire tracks, and downed trees it was clear Roach and Stitch hadn't left without a fight.

Whisper jerked off his back and hopped off the motorcycle. "What happened?"

He set the bike against a stump and got off. "There was a firefight." Careful to avoid the tracks, he stepped lightly to the edge of the disturbed dirt. "Looks like our enemies came through the forest. From the lack of downed trees, they must have been riding sand rails or something smaller."

Whisper shook her head. "If they were just little attack vehicles, Roach would have been able to fight them off."

Swash had been in enough battles to know better. "He'd have been behind the wheel where he could drive getaway. Even if he could work the rooftop cannon and Stitch could make it to the plasma cannon, it still would have been only two against"—he counted the tire tracks—"eight fast-moving pursuers."

"So they made a run for it?" Whisper's hopeful tone was accompanied by her searching the area away from the tracks.

Swash stood up and looked at the crushed trunks. "Well, they took off in that direction. Whether that was in an escape or as prisoners is hard to say."

Whisper fell to her knees. "I should have been here. I let my curiosity get the better of me, and now the rover and crew are gone."

The self-incrimination was a feeling he was well acquainted with, but it seldom served much purpose in a crisis. "Roach is the best driver I've ever worked with. If he couldn't evade them, there's not much either of us would have been able to do to help. Even though Stitch isn't the wiz you are at drone management, she would have been able to keep an eye on the raiders."

"Frack-water-sucking-drill-hole Blade!" Whisper left the expletive hanging in the air like a cloud of death beetles.

Swash couldn't disagree with her. The weapons master could well have proven the difference between a successful escape and their likely incarceration. "There's not much we can do about the past. We need to follow the tracks. At least we won't need the drones to know which way they were headed." At twenty-five tons and with eight-foot diameter tires, the trail the Beast cut wasn't exactly inconspicuous.

Whisper jumped up and started scanning the trees. "The drones."

"What are you thinking?" he asked.

She pointed toward a crook in the limbs. "Stitch, you sneaky little devil." Nestled in a crook between limb and trunk was one of the hummingbird drones.

Swash bolted toward the tree. With one good leap against the trunk, he snagged the ball of technology. He landed hard. "Okay, so we've got a bird with a busted wing. Now what?"

"Hand me your binoculars," she said.

"I don't understand what you're doing." He handed them over just the same.

She fished in the small center compartment between the

lenses for the connecting wire then plugged it into the drone. "This is one of my mother's new hummingbird drones. It records the last few minutes of what it sees. By crashing it into the tree, Stitch made sure the images didn't get recorded over." Whisper stared into the eye pieces and gave the ball a shake.

"What do you see?"

"Eight all-terrain mountain vehicles—that little six-wheeled hunting kind. The weapons mounted on the roll cages look military in origin."

"Is it your mother's forces?" Swash took the binoculars from her and tried to focus on the moving images.

"I don't think so," she said. "The trucks look too beat up. The armor is almost haphazard in what it covers. They look like marauders."

Swash pulled his eyes from the binoculars. "How do I reverse the playback?"

Whisper took the drone, held the bottom half, and rotated the top.

"Right." He went back to the video. "It could be Scorch's old crew. I'm not seeing his emblem though, so I doubt we're dealing with him—at least not directly. Eight vehicles with two mercenaries in each holding our rover and crew captive against just the two of us and that bike aren't the best odds, but I've dealt with worse." He took the binoculars and unhooked the drone. "There's nothing we can do here. The last time we heard from the Beast was before we entered the cave system for our return. That means at most they've got a six-hour lead on us."

Whisper headed back for the motorcycle. "But the Beast

doesn't move very fast, especially if Roach isn't on the run but is being forced to drive under threat."

Swash tried to run the figures in his head as he hopped back on the bike. "We should reach them in two hours if they're being held captive, three if Roach is on the run."

8

---

*B*lade woke up with the worst hangover he'd had all week, which was really saying something considering the life he'd been living in the gaming tower. He tilted his head and squinted as sunlight beamed through the glass wall. Time had little relevance when it came to drinking, whoring, and gambling, but the nearest he could figure it had to be late afternoon.

Laying naked across his stomach and snoring, Cypress still had hold of his cock like she was claiming it from the other prostitutes. If so, she had good reason. The daily orgy in Scorch's old penthouse—now Blade's domain—had left slumbering bodies strewn throughout the still swanky apartment.

He put his hand to his pounding forehead. Nothing seemed to make any difference to how he slept. Sober, his mind created detailed versions of his long-dead family. Each time the mental storyline unfolded, at their moment of destruction those he loved transitioned to the crew of the Beast. Falling asleep drunk or stoned only made the images more vibrant and disturbed. "I have to go after them."

Cypress squeezed his cock hard as she woke up. "What?" she grumbled with her face against the cushion.

He swatted her on her upturned rump. "The Beast. I'm going after it."

She finally let go of her prize and rolled to her side, forcing her weight into his already queasy gut. "Why?"

He wondered if all of the alcohol and sex had reduced her vocabulary to single word questions. "They're in trouble."

She rubbed her eyes as if seeing would help her better understand what he was saying. "How do you know?"

He stared at her like she'd never faced danger in her life, something he knew wasn't true. "How can they not be in trouble? They barely escaped destruction even with my help. And thanks to you, I've been too preoccupied to keep an eye on Scorch's old camp like I'd promised Swash. Those raiders are probably already in hot pursuit."

As she sat up off his body, his stomach rolled like a heaving ocean. "You're talking foolishness. I thought you agreed to staying here as your way to be free of those rovers."

She had a point. It took his brain a moment to process his emotions into thoughts. "Before he left, Swash told me that my connections to people had a sticky way of creeping up on me. Or something like that."

She frowned at him. "So those fools are like nutrogum stuck to your shoe? You don't yank that stanky stuff off and put it back in your mouth. Look around you. You've traded up."

He grasped her thigh and pulled his body into a seated position on the rumpled room-size mattress. "It's been a little over a week, and I'm already bonding to you. If I stay here, things will get ugly. They always do."

She rocked a little unsteadily as she squeezed her eyes shut then opened them again. "Two things. First, Warlord Inferno made it clear that if you leave her camp you'll walk out of here with only the clothing on your back. It's going to be a long hunt if you intend on crossing the high desert on foot. You'll be the one needing rescue. Second, if you leave, what happens to me?"

He couldn't fault her for her focus on self-preservation. "Let's deal with your situation first since that's obviously your biggest concern. The rule of the wild is that in any battle the loser's slaves become the property of the victor. You belonged to Scorch before you got here, making his contract on you one of the wild's and not the warlord's. Swash beat Scorch, or at least drove him off. Since Swash left his winnings to me, technically you're my slave regardless of where we are. I'm claiming possession. So you can either come along with me or jackrabbit to Inferno. If you leave me, however, I'll see to it that every credit I leave behind is used to keep you in the sex slave arena."

She crossed her legs and set her elbows to her knees. "Why do you insist on turning nasty? You don't need to threaten me."

His head was still pounding, and her tone wasn't

helping. "I'm sorry." Even to him, the tone didn't sound convincing.

Fortunately, her nod indicated she'd take what she could get. "And my first concern? You must have a plan for getting across the desert. And even if you succeed, are you really going to return to being an indentured servant to your old captain? If you do, he might assert his claim to me as his slave."

Just like a woman to start adding to her list of concerns. Blade checked the room to make sure all of the guests were still comatose. "I'm not going back to being a member of his crew." His mind was working through the plan much faster than he expected. "We're going to take one of Scorch's trucks—one that has living accommodations. It'll have to be heavily armed, but light enough to move fast. Fortunately, Inferno trusted me with inventorying the camp."

Cypress frowned and shook her head. "Those vehicles must all be sold off by now."

He struggled to focus on the dining room table in the next room and the computer pad he'd tossed onto the middle of it days ago. "I never turned in my report."

She unwrapped her arms and legs from their knot of disapproval and laid on her side—giving him a good show of her naked body. "Keep talking."

Working on the plan helped clear his brain from its alcohol-induced fog. "What happened to that electric-hybrid attack truck you drove during the race?"

She shrugged, swaying her sagging breasts. "Same as the truck you were riding in—returned to its owner."

Blade nodded as much to get his brain fully in gear as in

agreement. The trucks had only been loaners from marauders as their way of paying off debts owed to Blade. "Do you think honoring the rental agreement would have bought us any goodwill with the gamblers?" He could have just as easily claimed the vehicles as his own for being such an instrumental part of the race, but what he really needed was an attack force.

"Rovers and raiders settle on this camp and dissipate back into the wild as regularly as Inferno's disinfecting mist. I think we're better off taking what you're owed from Scorch's old camp and hightailing it out of here in secret rather than relying on a bunch of transients for support. The fewer people who know what we're up to the better."

He'd already used the stick to get her onboard, but a little carrot never hurt to seal the deal. "Inferno might not see our pilferage as justified. Me taking all of these women and strong-arming Scorch's old squad to join us would take time. I think you're right. Light and mobile would work better than heavily armed and easily tracked."

She arched her breasts toward him. "So, just you and me with a badass rover? I like it."

He looked around, wondering where his clothes had been tossed this time. "Take only what you need. To make this work, we're going to have to move fast."

BLADE STROLLED through the bad part of the trading camp like he was the one in charge and not Warlord Inferno. The powerful woman had an iron grip on the respectable parts of town and her fingers in the black market. When it came to the danger-riddled neighborhoods along the edge of the old city, however, she seemed happy to let the survival of the fittest rule. Blade had quickly established himself as the big-bad when it came to the murderers and thieves, but unlike Scorch, his influence wasn't achieved through intimidation. Everyone needed entertainment, and thanks to inheriting the trader's inventory, Blade had the best prostitutes in the city—as well as control of nearly every gambling den. All he'd had to do was run a reasonably honest and fair establishment. Other than alcohol and drugs, which Warlord Inferno controlled, if someone was in search of satiating their vice-riddled desire, he was the one they turned to. In only a little over a week—along with drinking, gambling, and whoring—he'd turned Scorch's den of thieves into an honest house of ill-repute. "I'm going to miss this place." He wondered if turning his back on so much potential was such a good idea. "Fracking Swash and his crew. My time with them must have infected me with a case of honorability."

Cypress pressed her hip to his butt. "I know where that can be cured."

Her sexual overture failed to arouse him. "After a week of your attempts at healing me, I'm inclined to think my affliction might be terminal." Unfortunately, his notoriety also made him highly visible. At the trader's bar, he leaned in toward Cypress. "You know which one I want?"

"I'm not dense. You made me memorize every dent and section of peeled paint on the camper."

Though she could drive like a fiend, fight like a tiger, and perform sex like an acrobat, Cypress also had the annoying habit of frying his brain in liquid anger. "Just don't get caught."

She took the collar of his cape and pulled his face to hers. "And you don't go getting into a fight that will slow us down. I need to seduce a gasser into taking me back to the neutral zone. If you see me getting him all hot and bothered, it's just part of the plan. Got it?"

He really had no place to claim her sexual devotion to only him—at least not while he'd so recently used her in his gambling and whoring tower. "I'm not some foolish rover who falls for every prostitute in the trading post. Do what you've got to do. I'll find a poker game and wait for you. If you're more than an hour, though, I'll assume you fracked up your part of the plan."

"Always the sweet talker." She wiggled her ass as she pushed through the door ahead of him.

As she headed toward a throng of drunk rovers too foolish to realize this wasn't the bar they should be drinking in, he leaned against the counter. "High-grade and recirc over the rocks. And don't even think about serving me that dump water you usually have on hand."

The barmaid pulled out a discolored bottle from under the bar and set it in front of him before turning to the uniform glass jars of trading post alcohol. "I know what you like."

Blade splashed some of the recirculated water onto his palm, sniffed it, then gave it a taste. "You need to change your filters."

The woman held out the bottle of alcohol. "Do you want the drink or not?"

"Let me see the glass." One time being drugged in the camp was more than enough for Blade.

She nearly busted the cup slamming it on the counter. "I swear, you are the most high-maintenance customer I get in here."

After a quick sniff to be sure it didn't smell like medicine, he handed it back to her. "What's the word among the junk miners?"

She carefully poured the water out of the dingy bottle to keep any sediment at the bottom. "They're still afraid to climb the dome. After your friends tore up the top layer, even a small puncture could release a fireball of methane. If someone doesn't retrieve those gas-bladders soon, the fuel stations are going to start running dry."

Blade had run a gasser once while running with his old band of marauders. The motors stunk, but they'd run on almost any petrol-methane mixture. "Good thing they'll never run out of plastic to reprocess." Out of the corner of his eye, he spotted Cypress leaving with a tall rover who seemed to have forgotten how to walk fully upright. Blade downed the drink in one gulp then handed the cup back to the barmaid. "Which table is turning over the most credits?"

"Back corner." She mixed him up another drink. "Do you want me to forget the limit?" Though Warlord Inferno had strict rules regarding inebriation in her trading post, the farther Blade got from the respectable neighborhoods the less the laws were enforced.

"That won't be necessary today. I'll be good." He took his

drink and strolled toward the poker table like an old-fashioned gunslinger ready for a fight.

"Blade." The dealer kicked the empty wooden chair out from under the table. "You don't often grace my game with your esteemed presence."

He took the chair and set it crossways to the table. "I felt like slumming it. Deal me in on the next round." He activated his credit pad and set it on the table then stretched his legs out past the back of the neighboring chair. "How's the action?"

"Settling into a routine. I suppose I should thank you for leaving Scorch's old camp intact." The dealer turned back to his cards. "Without their leader, those marauders have been pissing away most of their earnings."

Blade took one look at the other players and knew from their expressions who was about to go all-in, fold, or bluff. No matter what hands the others were holding, the dealer would end up taking the pot, one way or another. Some games were so predictable they became boring. "So all of the former marauders are now growing fat and content? From what I hear, you were one of them not long ago. You don't miss the dangerous wilds, dealing in slaves, and working a trading post until you had to hightail it out?"

The dealer shrugged and tossed two cards on the table. He took the replacements from the bottom of the deck while the others were focused on what to discard. "Scorch is an animal. With the Beast out there roaming the wilds, he'll have someone to hunt. I'm not big on getting caught in the middle of a vendetta. A year from now, maybe less, Scorch will come rolling through here again. Once I best who those marauders eventually put in charge, I'll build up his old camp. Then I'll either face off against Scorch for control or let him reward me for looking after his interests. It's really a no-lose situation for me." With all of the bets in, the guy tossed his cards on the table as if his winning was a foregone conclusion.

For the next three-quarters of an hour, hand after hand Blade split his victories with the dealer. The guy was a cheat, and not a very stealthy one. The trick was to keep the realization from the other players until the opportune moment. When the tall rover who had left with Cypress came stumbling back into the bar, Blade secreted his credit pad off the table.

By tapping on the pad with his fingers, he attracted the attention of the player next to him right when the dealer was palming an exchange of cards.

"You fracking-drill-rig cheat!" The man jumped to his feet, tossing the chair behind him.

Around the room, blasters and knives were drawn. Blade waited until the dealer lurched to his feet before he hit the ground. The action was like waving a starting flag to a line of racers. Stashing his credit pad into his cloak, Blade used the quickly escalating fight as a diversion to jackrabbit for the door.

Cypress swung the ungainly red truck with the flaming Earth logo on the hood against the sidewalk. "This one?"

He wrenched the door open and shoved her over to the passenger side. "What took you so long?" Hammering the accelerator, he leaned the vehicle back onto the street.

"That drunk rover was more coherent than I anticipated.

Is this your idea of a stealthy exit?"

He activated the roof-mounted plasma cannon. "I suppose I should have mentioned that I'm more the improvisational type than a preplanner. You might want to hang onto something."

"Please tell me you're not going to do what I think you're going to do." She brought her legs up to her chin and hung on tightly to the handle above the door.

"Just creating a little distraction." He lifted the gun headset from the sun visor and put it over one eye. Spotting a methane bladder sitting high and bloated on the edge of the dump dome, he gave it a quick blast of plasma. The initial explosion rocked the truck and set off blaring alarms throughout the trading post. With the accelerator hammered to the floor, the rig barely managed to keep ahead of the growing fireball.

"This is your idea of a distraction? Warlord Inferno is going to hunt you down with everything she's got, and if that doesn't work she'll put a bounty on your head so high even I might be tempted to collect."

Blade checked the rear camera. "Without Scorch's fleet of long-range trucks, she'll have a tough time catching us." He cast an appraising glare at Cypress. "And if you even think of betraying me, I'll enforce my full rights as master."

She settled back into the worn passenger seat and put her feet on the dashboard. "I'd like to see you try."

He wasn't sure if that was a threat or an invitation. As they headed onto the open desert, he knew every foot and tire in camp would be heading full speed toward the growing conflagration.

9

*R*oach gripped the steering wheel of the Beast with such ferocity that his knuckles turned white. With a marauder sitting in the observation chair and aiming a blaster at his head, he had little choice other than following the all-terrain buggy zipping through the desiccated forest ahead of the Beast. "Where are you taking us?" Roach needed to get the frack hole talking if he was to figure a way out of their predicament.

"To collect our bounty."

Scorch. The trader was the only one who had enough credits and anger to bother putting a price on the Beast and its crew. "Do you really trust that jackrabbit? You know he turned tail the moment he realized he was going to lose that race, right? What makes you think he's going to honor your contract?"

"That's not really your concern. Just drive the rover."

Roach plowed the Beast into a rotting tree trunk. *Why can't I find those damn death beetles now?*

The goon fell forward from the impact. "Watch where you're going."

Roach got the steering back under control. "This twenty-five-ton monster isn't as maneuverable as those little hunting vehicles your friends are driving. It would help if you'd let Stitch back on the bridge. She can run the drones to show me what's ahead." *And maybe point out a tree of death.* With Stitch's new inoculations, Roach hoped to use one of the only advantages they still had over their abductors.

"Just follow the lead and you'll be fine."

Roach doubted the guy had the authority to make any meaningful decisions. If he was going to get Stitch out of confinement in the crew quarters, their guard was going to need a little more incentive. The miniature truck ahead ducked hard left to avoid a hole left by the upturned roots of a dead tree. With his foot, Roach covertly shoved the lever that disengaged the front tires from the multifuel engines and laid into the accelerator with the other foot. He only turned the wheel of the Beast a quarter turn, dumping the front tire hard into the ditch and plowing the front catwalk into the dirt.

The guard lifted his blaster. "Get us out of this hole."

"I'm trying." With a hard spin of the steering wheel and a sharp burst of power from the engines, he heard the satisfying snap from under the rig. The Beast fell forward, bending the metal walkway on the ash-coated soil.

The guy jumped out of his chair and pressed the gun muzzle against Roach's head. "What did you do?"

Roach let go of the wheel and lifted his hands. "I did exactly what you told me to do. I did warn you that without eyes in the sky, maneuvering this rover is like driving a locomotive."

The guard looked out the view screen at his comrades. All eight little vehicles crowded around the front of the Beast like a swarm of angry wasps. He shook his gun as if that made it more menacing. "I told you to get us out of here."

Roach turned the driver's chair and leaned back. "That's going to be a little hard with a busted axle."

"Do something," the goon yelled.

"You're the one in charge, and with that gun in my face I'll do whatever you say. Maybe you should go talk to your boss."

With the burly dude climbing over the crumpled stairs of the Beast's catwalk, it wasn't hard to identify who was really in charge. "I wouldn't want to be you right now," the guard growled.

"Why aren't we moving?" The yell filled the crew quarters and resonated through the bridge hatch.

The guard backed to the doorway still shaking his gun at Roach. "He broke the axle."

The big man muscled his way past his henchman. "I thought I put you on this rig to make sure that didn't happen."

The guard held the gun at his side like a limp dick. "This rig isn't as maneuverable as our little buggies. How was I to know he couldn't make the corner? If you'd have let his assistant stay on the bridge, she could have run the navigation drones. I was just doing what you told me to do."

The man in charge turned back toward the guy standing next to the hatch. The guard never saw the big man's fist until it landed against his cheek and jaw. His head bounced off the thick metal wall before his body crumpled to the floor. "How long will it take for you to fix the axle?" he growled at Roach.

Having already replaced the metal rod once, Roach had a pretty good idea of what was involved, but he doubted the angry dude had any clue how long it might take. Roach needed every minute he could wrangle out of the frack hole if he was going to find Swash. "A day, maybe two. I won't know until I get under the rig and assess the damage."

"You've got an hour."

Roach folded his arms over his chest. "It'll take that long just to dig out the front of the Beast."

The head marauder hammered his heel against the floor hatch beside the driver's chair. "And I'm supposed to assume this is just for decoration? Get your scrawny ass under this rig and get to work. You just saw how I dealt with my subordinate's failure. Don't imagine that you'll fare any better than that lump on the floor just because there's a bounty on your head."

Roach got out of the driver's seat. "I need Stitch up here on the bridge. She's going to have to work the controls while I'm dislodging the axle. I'll also need my tool bag from the engine room."

"Fine." The man leaned down and yanked the guard's

weapon from his motionless hands. He then kicked the spineless fool on his way to the crew quarters. "I'll have the replacement guard bring you your purse after I send your little friend back to the bridge."

Facing a contingent of sixteen marauders, Roach wasn't in a position to mount a counterattack even if he could locate a weapon. His best chance at rescue was to wait for Swash. With any luck, he'd only be an hour or two behind.

Stitch tripped over the unconscious guard. She made a quick check behind her. "What are we going to do?"

Roach stared into her eyes, willing her to understand his deceptions. "Exactly what we're told. I'm going under the Beast to work on the axle, and you're going to operate the rig." Even with the big man outside barking orders to his troops, Roach couldn't be sure if someone might be listening. The guard on the floor looked sufficiently knocked out, but that wasn't an assumption Roach was willing to rely on.

"You're the one in charge," Stitch said.

He kind of wished she hadn't reminded him. For his first time officially in command of the Beast, his reign had been one of foolish inattention. He should have had every drone the two of them could manage covering the area. Even though Stitch would have insisted on focusing their attention on Swash and Whisper—waiting desperately to hear some word on what was happening—at least the stationary drones would have alerted them to the oncoming attack. He hadn't even heard the marauders' vehicles until they were right in front of the Beast. Playing Whisper's music for Stitch to pass the time had been fracked-up stupid. At least the marauders had taken the Beast before Stitch could get to the guns. If she'd have been behind the controls of the weapon, they'd have sliced her in two with their blasters. "Take the driver's seat. Do what I tell you and nothing else. Whatever happens out there, we need to stay focused on the repair."

Another guard entered the bridge carrying Roach's agroleather tool bag. He dropped it next to the hatch before unshouldering his weapon. "Don't do anything stupid."

Stitch bit her lip and nodded as if the ideas for rescue were forming in her mind. Taking the driver's seat, she inspected the control settings. "Multifuels are still running." She nudged the front wheel disconnect with her shin and frowned her question at him.

He couldn't imagine that the guard with the gun would be able to guess what the forward thrust lever was designed for or when it had been disengaged. But that didn't mean he wanted to inadvertently give the frack hole a lesson on the Beast's controls. He gave Stitch a quick half nod to confirm her suspicion as he opened the floor hatch and put his feet on the short ladder. "Once I'm in position, you'll need to back the Beast up. The hole under us isn't big enough to work on the axle and access this hatch at the same time. You'll be sealing me down there." He grabbed the tool kit and descended into the darkness. Even with the Beast jammed into the Earth, he could see the damage was exactly as he'd intended. The breakaway joint had performed its function better than he'd imagined possible when he installed it during the refit.

"The boss wants to know how it looks." The guard loomed over the hatch with his gun aimed at Stitch.

"Busted in two," Roach said. "I need Stitch to back the Beast up a few feet. I'll yell when it's in the right position."

As the rover pulled dirt into the hole, he watched the tire, hatch, and gap next to the upturned tree root all at the same time. When no light could be seen through the hatch and the edge of the Beast ground against the bottom of the tangle of wood, he hollered for her to stop. "This is precision work, so don't expect me to be giving you minute-by-minute updates," he yelled.

"I suppose you're not going anywhere." The guard's voice was muffled by the small gap between the ground and the bottom of the Beast.

Roach made a show of rattling the tools as he unloaded them and grumbling about the tight working conditions. "Turn the steering straight," he yelled.

As Stitch lined up the tires, the disconnect reengaged. With his stated job complete, Roach checked the gaps around the undercarriage. In front of the Beast, he counted the tire footprints of all eight attack vehicles as well as the feet of every marauder except the two on the bridge. Though the gap under the hatch was barely large enough for him to slip his hand into, the angle against the tree provided a little more room. It would still be too tight for a human to slip through—making it appear to be a non-threat to the men standing guard—but Roach wasn't exactly human in dimensions.

He eased back into the hole then shed his daily driving outfit and fake bodysuit. In only his leotard, he could easily wiggle under the Beast, but that might not be enough to secure his escape. He needed to divide the enemy force if Swash was going to have any hope of going up against the marauders.

The Beast had her secrets, and as Swash's second in command, Roach had been made privy to one of the most well-kept. He squirmed down the overlapping metal plates that protected the batteries and floor of the rover. When he reached a spot under Whisper's radio nook, he felt around for the secret panel. He'd only been allowed to play with the Beast's secondary operations station once while Stitch and Whisper were practicing their weapon's training, but that had been enough. When the computer screen popped down, so did the remote control for the jump spider that he'd hidden in the compartment. He pulled out the emergency blaster and stashed it under a strap of the leotard.

To keep the Beast from being commandeered, the operational computer screen was hardwired to the systems and only provided simple controls, but he wasn't interested in moving the rover. Bringing up the rear diagram of the Beast, he activated the louvered rear blast shield that protected the jump spider. Tapping the screen, he freed his little sand rail from the rover.

The jump spider's remote was considerably less sophisticated, but more to Roach's tastes. Working his fingers on the levers while watching the small view screen, he fired up the small engine then sent a cloud of ash and dust so dense it blocked out the view of the Beast.

Engines roared to life in front of the rover. Commands were yelled. And finally, tires tore up the ground in hot pursuit. He counted six of the eight all-terrain vehicles as they screamed down the hill after the remote-control buggy. He angled the jump spider away from the direction the Beast had traveled. Swash would certainly be following the path of destruction left by the twenty-five-ton rover.

While continuing his manipulation of the controls, he snuck out from under the Beast. *Now I just need to find Swash before these fools realize I'm not in the jump spider.*

10

*W*hile following the Beast's tracks, Swash envisioned all manner of disasters that he might come upon. His crew—for he couldn't stand to think of the duo as his first mate and lover—bound, tortured, or worse. His rover bombed, dismantled, or flying Scorch's vile flaming Earth sigil. Finding his enemy looming over his possessions seemed like a foregone conclusion.

What he did not expect to find was Roach out of his fake-body disguise leaning against a boulder while playing with what appeared to be a video game. "What the hell?" Swash yelled as he pulled on the motorcycle's brakes.

Whisper was off the back of the bike before it fully came to a stop. She ran so fast it looked like she was flying. The impact of bodies sent the remote control flying to the ground. "I thought I'd lost you."

Locked in Whisper's embrace, Roach looked at Swash and pointed at the metal box. "You have to keep the jump spider moving. If those fools realize I'm not behind the wheel, they'll come barreling back toward the Beast."

Swash dropped the motorcycle and dove for the joysticks. Though he'd never played with Roach's contraption, he'd spent enough time on remote commands to understand the basics. The dust-caked image on the view screen jumped and crashed as the sand rail came back under his control. "What are we dealing with?"

Roach managed to extricate his body from Whisper's hold. "I've got six of the eight minitrucks on my buggy's ass. The other two are probably still stationed in front of the Beast. One of the raiders was comatose when I left, leaving three watching Stitch. She's safe, but she won't be if they figure out what I'm doing."

"How far are we?" Swash struggled to keep the jump spider zipping through the dead forest while planning the rescue.

"Less than a mile." Roach gently took the box back from Swash.

With Roach safe, Swash turned his full attention to protecting Stitch. "Whisper, I'm relying on your communications expertise. I need to contact the Beast without anyone figuring it out. It might also be nice if we could finally turn the tables on these frackers. With what you've got in front of you, can we hack into their conversations?"

She rushed to the downed bike and pulled out the case of com links. "First things first. When you say the Beast, I assume you mean Stitch. If I take the busted hummingbird drone to a spot overlooking the rover, she might be able to hear us, but she'd have to be wearing a com."

"I did not say Stitch," Swash said. "I said the Beast. Get that hummingbird in position then line up our coms. Once you've done that, turn your attention to breaking into these marauders' communication network."

She grabbed her stuff then lifted the bike from the ground. "I'll be right back."

As she zoomed off, Swash looked over Roach's shoulder at the view screen. "Who are they?"

Roach shrugged his narrow monkey shoulders. "They're not Scorch's crew, but he's probably not far off. They were taking us to him."

Swash figured as much. "If he's involved, those mercenaries will know they didn't get all of us. So long as they've got one of us in the trap, they'll assume we'll come back for a rescue. And if Scorch is nearby, it's a good bet his goons will want to join in the fun."

"And here I thought I was helping by dividing their force." Roach angled the controller as the image from the jump spider tilted a full ninety degrees from horizontal.

"You did great. I just need to figure out how to capitalize on the advantage you gained us before we lose it."

"What the fracking hell is that?" Roach held up the controller. The jump spider was headed straight for a decent-sized red rover with a flaming Earth logo painted on the hood.

"Scorch!" Swash's blood ran hot. If only he was in the jump spider instead of watching the view screen, he could confront the bastard before he approached Stitch inside the Beast.

"I don't think so, boss." Roach magnified the image. "Look at the driver. Tell me that doesn't look like Blade."

BLADE HAD EXPECTED A FIGHT. He just didn't think it would be coming straight at him. "Power up the plasma cannon but don't shoot until I say so. And whatever you do, don't hit the jump spider."

"I'm not stupid." Cypress extended the targeting screen from the dashboard to between her thighs. The action brought forth joysticks with firing triggers from the armrests. "I was a pretty important part of keeping your friends safe out on that desert run if you'll remember. I know the jump spider when I see it." She stared at the screen. "But you might like to know, there's no one at the controls."

Blade smiled. "Roach must have finished the remote-control operations we were working on. That... dude"— Blade stopped himself from calling Roach a gen mod at the last second—"has some mad skills. He must be running a diversion tactic. Hold your fire until I get a better look at what's going on."

"Yes, sir." Her insolent tone was something he'd have to deal with eventually. How Scorch had managed to maintain his temper with the slave was beyond him. She leaned in closer to the cannon's view screen. "There's an awful lot of them out there. We're going to be swarmed like we've stepped into a hornet's nest." She made an exaggerated trigger motion with her finger.

"Lay off the firing control, and when I tell you, only shoot at what I say. I want to get as close as possible first. So long as they think we're part of Scorch's militia they won't attack."

She looked at him, fuming. "Or they already know about our theft of the truck and are just drawing us into a kill zone. Word travels fast across the high desert."

The six minitrucks fanned out like piranhas scoping out the best section of flesh to sink their teeth into. "Idiot number two on my left. Take him out with a single burst," Blaze said, knowing as the one farthest behind, his absence wouldn't be immediately noticed by the others more intent on their target.

The flash of light barely registered as more than a flick of the truck's high beams. With laser-like precision, Cypress hit the midsection of the open-air metal box on wheels. Cart and occupants tumbled backward away from the circling noose of vehicles. "Which one next?"

Blade spun the truck hard toward the gap in the attack force and hammered the accelerator just as the two lead vehicles opened fire on the jump spider. "Take out the one farthest away on your side."

She yanked hard on the left joy stick while pushing the other toward the dashboard. "For the love of life, why? I should be taking out the most dangerous ones."

"Do what I tell you." He swung around a boulder as she took aim across the field of dirt and dust. The blast exploded the fuel tank and lit up the dead forest.

"Dammit!" Blade turned the truck into the center of the disoriented all-terrain vehicles. "Now they'll jackrabbit on us. I needed them to think they had the edge so they wouldn't leave." Two of the minitrucks peppered Blade's rover with bullets, punching holes in systems under the hood that were going to need an expert to repair.

"How was I supposed to know what you were thinking? You could tell a girl, you know." She lowered the barrel and punched a hole through the closest vehicle. Its machine gun bounced off their truck's radiator.

The remaining three attackers headed for the tree line. "Take out the fool on the left before he gets behind the boulder."

Cypress's shot missed, cutting the massive rock in two. "Sorry."

"Don't apologize during a fight. So long as the cannon is swinging right, take out that fracker directly ahead."

She kicked the small vehicle right in the ass with her plasma ray, sending it end-over-end and smashing so hard into a desiccated tree that only bugs and splinters remained. "Only two left."

"Yeah, but where are they?" Blade followed the torn-up ground left by the sliding tires. "I just hope Swash's band of rovers aren't twiddling their thumbs. I'm afraid they're about to see the return of some unwanted guests."

11

---

*S*wash watched the battle unfold on the view screen like he was studying tactical maneuvers. Each feint, shot, and position that Blade undertook set him up for his next assault. The attack of one heavily armed truck against the six smaller and more versatile all-terrain vehicles was a thing of beauty. By all reckoning, Blade should have been brought down like a baby feral pig attacked by rats. Instead, due to his carefully taken shots, with each assault it was a minitruck that was put out of commission.

"Whisper's back," Roach said from his position in the tree limbs.

"About time." Swash handed back the control box. With Blade taking on the marauders, the jump spider had been useless in the fight and reduced to observer status. "You can retrieve your remote-control toy now."

Whisper pulled the black bike alongside Swash. "By

positioning the drone, I achieved direct contact with the Beast's communication system, but without Stitch wearing a com, I still don't see what good that's going to do you. You'll have to climb that knoll to see the drone." She handed over an earbud.

"And how did you do on cracking into our enemy's system?" he asked.

"Those guys are idiots. They're piggybacking on any system they find. I set up that earbud I handed you to hear them. Just switch the setting from *Direct Line of Contact* to *All Signals*, and you should hear every word they say."

He stuck the com in his ear. "Round up our gear. I want you and Roach to head for Blade on the sand flea."

"Blade's here?" Her excitement was impossible to miss.

"He's dealing with the marauders Roach distracted. I'm sure he'll have plenty of stories to regale you with later, but for now, we're in a battle. Best to keep your game face on. When you reach him, tell Blade what we're up against. If all goes well, I'll have the Beast on lockdown when he's ready to make his assault on the camp."

"Right, Captain."

"What about the jump spider?" Roach yelled.

"Keep it coming my way. I'll use it to get to the Beast. Together with Blade, we should be able to pin down the remaining marauders."

Swash climbed the small hill as Roach and Whisper sped off on the motorcycle. He looked around to make sure there wasn't even a rat to overhear his communication. "Earth rover Beast, this is your captain, Swashbuckler Jones. Confirm."

"Voice imprint confirmed." The robotic female voice had all the warmth of a granite boulder.

"Situation report. List occupants and their locations."

"The Beast is in invader lockdown status. Medical Officer Stitch is confined to her bunk. One enemy guard remains unconscious on the bridge while a second is standing watch behind the driver's station. Without a member of the crew on deck, I've disabled the bridge's command center."

"So the goons are on the bridge?"

"Question exceeds my parameters."

Frack. He closed his eyes to remember the computer's limited vocabulary. Every order had to be made as a statement. The computer didn't understand the complexity of being questioned. "Confirm that there are two invaders isolated to the bridge."

"Confirmed."

"Close and seal bridge hatch, then reconfirm previous inquiry."

A moment passed that felt way too long—certainly enough time for a marauder standing guard to escape through the slowly closing hatch. "Two invaders remain on the bridge. Hatch is closed and dogged. Lock engaged."

Good girl. Swash breathed a little easier. "Close and lock all external hatches."

The response came much faster this time. "The Beast is secure."

"Status of Medical Officer Stitch's berth."

"Closed and locked."

"Unlock Medical Officer Stitch's berth." He felt like he

was talking to an idiot, but without basing the Beast's computer interface on artificial intelligence, he had to rely on the most basic of commands to be understood.

"Lock disengaged."

"Connect me to Medical Officer Stitch's berth."

"What's going on?" Stitch asked.

"Sorry," he said, grateful to be talking to a human again. "It took me a minute to get control of the situation. Are you okay?"

"Oh, I'm just wonderful. I love being manhandled then thrown in my bunk like a petulant little girl."

He understood her outrage. After being freed from captivity, the rush of anger was one he'd experienced before. "We're not out of the woods yet. The bridge is sealed with your captives inside, and the Beast is locked tight. How many are left outside?"

"Last I saw there were two vehicles and two goons. One of them is the guy in charge. You won't be able to miss him. Just look for the biggest pile of shit you run across. How are the others?"

He didn't see any point in hiding Blade's arrival since the marauders were already under his attack. "We had a little help. Blade and Cypress crashed Roach's little game of cat and mouse. I've got Whisper and Roach meeting up with our reunited friends. Together we'll make an attack to clean out the rest of your abductors. I'll have you out of there in less than half an hour. Just sit tight."

SWASH DIDN'T LIKE BEING out of control regarding the multitiered attack, but he didn't have much of a choice. At the edge of the clearing, he tossed the wounded drone high up in a tree. "Stitch, have you still got me?"

"I'm here. I'm always here. I can't see anything though, being cooped up in the crew quarters. At least I'm out of that bunk. You might have finally figured out a way to make me stay with you during our mutual sleep cycles."

"Just stay safe." He wanted to give her an idea of what was about to happen, but trusting communications links, even ones that should be secure, never ended well. He switched his com to *All Users*.

"What the fracked-up hell are we going to do now?" a voice yelled. "Scorch made it clear he wanted the crew, sand rail, and rover."

"Shut up," a second voice barked. "I don't pay you to tell me what I already know. Once the others get back, we'll take the Beast to Scorch. The rest of the crew are going to have a hard time surviving in only that little buggy. They'll follow us to their beloved rover like rabid little rat pups chasing after their momma."

"If you say so. What's taking those guys so long? How hard can it be for six mountain vehicles to chase down a sand rail?"

Swash had heard all he needed to. The two goons standing around the Beast were just wandering marauders out for a quick score with the West Coast trader. Using the jump spider's targeting visor, he swept the area around the Beast for the two idiots. They'd have to be far enough from the rover for the plasma burst to hit them but not the vehicle. He doubted he'd get a shot, but keeping watch like a sniper involved putting the odds of success aside.

He kept alert for any sound of the incoming all-terrain vehicles Blade was unable to destroy. But even focusing on his listening, he failed to pick up the electric motorcycle. A quick, staticky tap from his earbud was all the warning he received.

The black bike swished in from the tree line below Swash's observation post. Roach kept low over the handlebars.

"What the—" The hired hand's com went silent as a laser-tight burst of lightening erupted from Whisper's gun. Aiming over Roach's back, she lined up with the guy in charge. He didn't even get his blaster out of its holster before a blazing red hole appeared in his chest.

Swash leaned back in the driver's seat of the jump spider. He knew the girl had it in her to be the ruthless dealer of death, but seeing that potential come to fruition meant he'd have to reassess her worth and threat levels.

"Boss, if you're out there, Blade's herding in the remaining marauders. We could sure use those jump spider cannons." The high-pitched screech in Roach's voice betrayed both his concern and gen mod origins.

Swash tapped the com once in reply before firing up the small engine. Between Blade's roof-mounted arsenal and the buggy's cannons, dispatching the two remaining minitrucks would be as easy as swatting flies. Then they'd just have to deal with the two guards trapped on the bridge.

12

$\mathcal{A}$fter her service on Diablo Island, Stitch thought she'd finished putting in her time running interrogations. But questioning a pair of marauders who'd have been happy to kill her was considerably different than finding out if someone was secretly a gen mod. "What do you want me to do?" she asked Swash.

The captain sauntered around the two goons hog tied and strapped into two of the crew entertainment pods. "I need to know where Scorch is hiding, how big his crew is, and what he intended for us. And I need to believe the information is factual. What happens to these two gas-frackers after you have their stories doesn't matter to me."

Arguing for their lives would have been a waste of breath and probably would have earned her a reprimand. Whether he meant it or not, Swash clearly wanted the goons to think they could be down to their last hours on

Earth. "I've got some truth serum, and a vial of death-beetle plague if that doesn't work."

Swash leaned on the top of one of the pods and glared down at its occupant. "You two were just foot soldiers. Your boss is dead. You've screwed your mission. And you're not getting out of these mountains without help. I hope you fully appreciate your position, because I'm not spending all day waiting for your intel." He turned back to Stitch. "I'll be outside with the others. Do what you have to and let me know when you believe their stories."

Once he'd left, Stitch turned to her former guards. "I'm not in the habit of outright killing someone, but don't let that lull you into feeling safe. You see, I can't help myself from providing life-saving measures even if I've been the one to provide the threat to life. Do you understand?"

The pair slowly nodded with the gags still in their mouths. She ambled to her medical lab, allowing the goons time to process what had been said. Though she'd been given weapons training—and Swash had made it clear she may one day have to be responsible for killing someone— she wasn't sure she'd be able to take the life of anyone not pointing a weapon at her or those she loved. She prepared eight syringes, four for each of the goons. In addition to the truth drug, vile of death, and antidote, she took out her sleeping concoction. If they thought they were drifting off, they might well believe this was their end.

She wasn't even sure all of the preparations were justified. Swash was right. They had no reason to hide anything. Though when it came to espionage, he was far more skilled at it than she was. The goons might be playing a long game in a foolish attempt to turn the tables on the Beast's crew after they'd made it to some spot designated by Scorch for an emergency ambush. *I'm starting to think like Swash.*

She rolled up the needles in a towel and headed back toward her patients. The two remained stoically defiant in their stares. "I'm starting you off with the truth serum. I'm sure you've had some version of it before. Fight the effects and you'll get massive headaches. Tell me what I want to know, and we can get this done fairly quickly." She held up the rolled towel. "Be difficult and we will do this the hard way. You have no value to us beyond your information on Scorch." She pulled out their gags then spun the two pods away from each other. If they were as clever as Swash suspected, she didn't need them being tricky. With two good firm jabs, she had them drugged up.

She started with the one who'd had his face bashed in by his boss. "I'd guess you've already got a pretty good pounder going on inside that cranium. Lie to me, and I might be dealing with a burst hematoma. Though I could use the challenge of brain surgery, saving your life would take time I'd rather not waste. Let's start with something easy. Where's Scorch?"

"Up your ass." His teeth clinched as his eyes looked like they were about to pop out of his head.

"Now, was that a smart answer? Let's go again. Where's Scorch?"

"Ten miles along the ridge toward the New Mormon territory." Though the blood vessels still bulged around the whites of his eyes, he no longer looked to be in mortal peril.

"One respectable answer, one break in the action. Don't go anywhere. I suspect your companion might be a little quicker with his truth."

"I'm not telling you anything, you medical whore." The pod behind the one she leaned against rocked side to side.

She picked up the towel and its contents then walked around to the other victim. "I don't actually expect that you will." She unrolled the towel far enough to extricate one of the syringes. "Here's your problem. I doubt you know anything more than your friend, and he's already shown some flexibility in his allegiance. I really only need one of you. Killing you just might push mush-face over the edge. So I'm not even going to ask you a question. Either you start talking, or this concoction of fast-acting death-beetle virus gets pushed into your vein. It's not a pretty death."

His eyes locked onto the glass cylinder like he could see the pathogen just waiting to infect his organs. "Okay, just put that thing down. It's a trap. The truth is, we don't know where Scorch has his camp. We were told to get you into a box canyon ten miles north. From what I saw, he must have twenty men with him. That's all I know. I swear. It's not like Scorch was going to confide in any of us. We were just a small raiding force. Our boss knew these mountains, so Scorch used us to hunt you down. Once we turned you over to him, he said we'd be welcome to visit the territory. We've been a long time out in these wastelands."

"Now where would he get a force like that?" Stitch asked as much to herself as her prisoner. "When he jackrabbited out of Inferno's camp, it was just him and his truck."

"Lady, there's a reason he's edging you closer to the New

Mormons. A guy like Scorch isn't going to keep his full force in one location. Are you really dumb enough not to realize he's got outposts in the North?"

She considered jabbing him with the needle out of sheer annoyance. Instead she gave the plunger a slight push, dribbling a couple of drops onto the dude's leg. "So Scorch simply wants to kill us all? Where's the sport in that?"

He pressed hard into the pod as if that would somehow prevent the fluid from soaking through his agroleathers. "I'm telling you I have no idea what he wants."

She jabbed the needle into his leg and gave him the full dose of sleeping potion. Without waiting for the other goon to plead his case, she performed the same action on her other captive. With both of them knocked out cold, she activated her private connection to Swash and gave him her report.

13

---

*B*lade had been looking forward to his conversation with Swash and dreading it at the same time. Like going up against a world-class poker player, he could walk away with his heart's desire or be left slinking out of the game without even his shirt. The biggest difference between the talk and the game was Swash's intellect and honesty. Blade would have to win his arguments on their merit, not on bluster.

"So you're back. I suppose this means I owe you one." Swash was a hard man but fair. "You must realize we're not done with Scorch just yet. So what are you after? What would keep you by my side through the upcoming battle?"

Unlike playing the gambling dealer back in Inferno's camp, Blade would have to start off by laying his proverbial cards on the table. "With that truck I commandeered and Cypress as my crew, I now captain my own rover. We won't be subject to your authority. Clearly, the Beast is far better equipped. So it will be up to you to provide food, fuel, and drone support. In return, I'll supply you with the tactical advantage you've been missing. With us no longer shackled together by the limitations of only one vehicle, I'll be able to scout the areas we drive through."

"So a long-term commitment." Swash set his foot on a large rock and leaned his forearms on his knee. "We won't always be dealing with Scorch. There's a lot of land and dangers out there. Dividing the chores means our survival is only part of what's involved in traveling together. What are your thoughts on where we head?"

Honestly, Blade didn't care where they went, so long as he could outrun his nightmares. "You're the one with the mission. I won't dispute anywhere you want to go. And if I don't like your leadership, Cypress and I will be on our way. I'm not looking for another binding contract. My one requirement is that during a battle, I'm the one in charge. I can't be consulting you on tactics."

Swash nodded. "While my people are on board the Beast, they are under my command, but during an attack, I will deploy my vehicle as you see fit."

Blade played his final card. "One last issue. I'm not calling you captain, not unless you do likewise."

"Captain Blade?" Swash rubbed the stubble on his chin. "I can live with that."

"I like the sound of it." Using the formal titles for each other beat having to constantly call the man Swash.

"What do you propose we do about Scorch?"

Time to get down to work. Though Blade had bristled under Swash's command, he'd always appreciated the man's ability to focus on the challenge ahead. They both had a score to settle with the West Coast trader. "If we don't face him soon, he'll just flame up again like a methane blow hole —better to deal with him as a united front."

"You realize he's drawing us into the New Mormon territories? In spite of her past, Whisper is on board with returning to her one-time captors. But my understanding is Cypress might find the community one she'd like to avoid."

Blade kept his cold smile from touching the sides of his eyes. "I can deal with my own crew."

Swash pushed off the rock. "We have an accord. While out in the wilds, we'll work together to survive. In battle, you call the shots. And when we're in camps, we'll respect each other as fellow rover captains." He held out his hand.

Blade didn't care much for complex agreements, so this one suited him just fine. He shook Swash's hand. "If we're going after Scorch, that puts me in charge. Make sure you're okay with that, because this is your last chance to back out. Once we're rolling, you'll have to drive that rover where I say and position your crew as I want."

"Just don't go getting us all killed. Do you have a tactic in mind?"

Blade looked back at his rig. "Well, I am driving one of his old vehicles, and you've got one of his electric motorcycles. We could make it look like I was bringing you in for the reward. Even if he blames me for the trouble he created in Warlord Inferno's camp, he might see me bringing you in as a peace offering."

Swash looked suspicious. "Or you could *actually* be hauling us in. You did kind of just swoop in out of nowhere.

By knocking off the marauders, you'd be in a prime position to collect the bounty."

Blade had to respect Swash's protective instincts, even if they would have served him better at the beginning of the negotiation rather than after it had been concluded. "I'm not in league with Scorch, and I'm not interested in collecting no damn bounty. If I'd have wanted credits, I'd have stayed in the trading camp. But the fact that you're suspicious of my intent proves that the ruse should work on Scorch as well."

WITH NEGOTIATIONS CONCLUDED, Swash put his com back in and set it so he could be heard by both crews. "Everyone, stow what you're working on and meet me and Captain Blade in front of the Beast."

"Please tell me you're not pulling one of your debate forums again." Blade glared at Swash. "I don't want to have to defend my edicts to your crew."

"I'm not. As captain of the Beast, I make the decisions on where she goes. But just because I make the decisions, that does not mean I jump into something without getting all of the input that's appropriate." Swash had never really been a *new* captain. Having grown up with his grandfather at the wheel and then serving as second in charge under his father, by the time he took the helm of the Beast he more than knew what he was doing. Blade, however, had just had the keys handed to him with no clue as to how to deal with subordinates. Swash resigned himself to the idea that he was going to have to play mentor to the disagreeable weapons master—even if neither one of them liked the idea.

"I still think it's foolish. A crew shouldn't believe they can dictate what a captain does."

"Mine don't." Swash turned away from Blade as the others emerged from around the rover. "We're going after Scorch," he announced when he had their attention.

Stitch leaned against the front of the rover. "That's going to put us really close to the New Mormon territories. The goons bound in the crew pods said they were supposed to lure us into a trap, and Scorch has regrouped with his contingent from the north. This isn't going to be a matter of hunting down one guy in a truck with a minimal force at his command."

Swash didn't really need the update. He'd been wearing his com, and even though Stitch hadn't, the Beast had other listening devices. He'd heard every word that had passed between Stitch and the goons. "I didn't say it was going to be easy."

Cypress stood at Blade's side. "You also didn't say it was going to be a suicide mission. I've been under that guy's control. He doesn't know how to surrender. Make no mistake; this will be a fight to the death. And though the contingent at the trading post stepped aside once you won the race, don't expect the same from the band he travels with."

"Has he changed that much from when we were slaves together?" Whisper asked.

"He's grown ruthless," Cypress replied.

Swash frowned at the two women. "Is this going to be a

problem for either of you? It's not just about going up against your former captor. One way or another, eventually we'll be dealing directly with the New Mormons. How are they likely to respond to our little war?"

Whisper stood ramrod straight, an indication she was thinking like a fighter and not the scared child she'd been when she was a slave to the religious cult. "No matter how those zealots feel about it, they won't leave their territorial boundaries. As I said before, I'm on board, Captain." She showed more enthusiasm than Swash thought appropriate, given her past.

"What aren't you telling me?" he asked.

She looked down at her moving foot as if it were writing the answer in the dust. "There was a reason my mother sold me to the New Mormons. The latest incarnation of Joseph Smith is a space whack job. He not only believes there are other inhabited planets, but also that living on them are other versions of ourselves."

"And he would need satellites to talk to them." Swash could see the puzzle pieces fitting together. No one was as single-minded as an evangelist.

"Something like that," Whisper said. "Most of what I know is stuff I figured out later in life—after I left the New Mormons. My mother might have set my feet on this path, but it's not like a military leader in charge of a secret mission is going to confide in her nine-year-old daughter-spy."

Swash usually took Whisper's ramblings with a degree of skepticism, but when she did make sense, it was often at the end of a long and hard series of experiences. "What conclusions did you come to?"

"The bottom line is that Joseph Smith VII has the territory, influence, and resources to be the one I'm after—or at least be the one who pulls the strings. My mother must have reached the same conclusion. As a girl, I had no way to confirm that suspicion, but being away from the territories gave me other perspectives on the New Mormons which helped me round out my impression. I've had some time to think about what we heard from Aural and Lemur. I think my mother's trying to draw a noose around Joseph Smith by having us check out all of these satellite installations. But that's not something I can back up with facts."

Swash hoped the noose didn't constrict around the Beast and her crew while trying to land Sky Payne's intended target. "And you're willing to risk facing your original owners to prove your hypothesis?"

She stood a little straighter. "On my own, no. With you and the rest of my... family—I can't come up with a more appropriate title—then yes. If your plan is to go after Scorch, that just means I won't be finagling you all into another dangerous mission for my benefit alone. As you said, one way or another, after facing Scorch we'll have to travel north. But you should know, I'm not as certain about Joseph Smith VII being the key master as I once was. He just seems too obvious. Still, I do believe he's my mother's ultimate target, and I've yet to find another candidate worth pursuing."

Swash turned slightly toward Cypress. "You're not a member of my crew, and I never claimed slaveholder status over you. So my question doesn't bind you to anything. I have heard your warning, but what are your honest feelings about crossing Scorch and ultimately Joseph Smith VII?"

Cypress tightened her grip on the blaster holstered at her side like she was ready to do battle right then and there. "Scorch is a lying, cheating piece of reconstituted shit. I won't shed a pussy tear when I see him carved up by a blaster. I might even like to take a slice at him myself. As for the New Mormons?" She looked at Blade as if assessing his worth as her champion. "I won't be going back to being a house servant. They didn't like me much. I was too lippy. Blade has seen the scars they left on me. If the intention of my captain is to go in, I don't have much option but to go along." She turned back toward Swash. "But if things go badly, I'll die before becoming one of the New Mormon slaves again."

He looked around at the small band. "Anyone have anything to add—ideas, concerns, suggestions? Now's the time. Once we face off against Scorch, win, lose, or run like hell, it's a safe bet we'll be crossing into the Northern Territories."

Roach reached up and patted the Beast's catwalk. "Sounds like impossible odds. I'm in."

"Where you go, I go." Stitch made her declaration with more emotion than Swash found comfortable hearing in public.

14

*B*ack behind the wheel where he belonged, Roach worked the Beast out of the desiccated forest and into a wide dusty valley devoid of vegetation. "What's your plan for those idiots in the back?" Having hostages didn't sit well with him, but turning them lose seemed like a mistake that might come back to bite them in the ass.

Swash kept watch on the hummingbird drones from the navigator's chair. "I've been giving that some thought. Technically, this is Blade's operation, but that doesn't mean I can't have a suggestion. Somewhere up ahead there's a trap waiting. We need to spring it before we roll our tires into an ambush. That means we're going to need a good convincing deception. Blade's idea is to have someone in blacked-out garb on the motorcycle in front while he drives his truck from behind. It'll look like he's bringing us in for the bounty. My idea is to rig those marauders up in the jump spider and run it on remote control. We need to make it look like they're outrunning our convoy. Scorch's biomed sensors will indicate that they are alive, but in full garb and wearing targeting helmets, he won't be able to identify who's in the buggy. He'll assume a couple of us are attempting an escape. Hopefully, his first line of defense will head off in pursuit of the sand rail, leaving the door open to our incursion. Scorch's guards that are left behind should be sufficiently appeased by Blade and shorthanded enough to not feel the need to poke around our rig and disarm us. We need to get inside of Scorch's defenses before we launch our attack. Ideally, I'd like to have a knife at the fracker's throat before he could raise the alarm."

"Sounds like more than just a suggestion. Who are you planning on putting behind the handlebars?" Even with the addition of Blade and Cypress, the plan seemed to stretch their resources to the breaking point.

Swash peered over at Roach. "You're the most logical choice. Blade is going to need Cy at weapons on the truck. I'll be at the Beast's controls. That leaves Whisper and Stitch to operate our weapons and play with the buggy's remote controls."

Roach wasn't crazy about being off the Beast during an operation, but Swash's assignments made the most sense. "And once we get behind Scorch's perimeter?"

Swash spread the drones for a wider but less detailed hologram of the area ahead. "The battle details I'll happily leave to our former weapons master."

"And after the battle?" Roach asked. "I've never known you to throw in your lot with another rover." Though Roach hoped for the best regarding the alliance, having the two men working together seemed like mixing nitric acid and glycerin together while hoping things didn't explode.

"Today, we need him. By now you should realize I stay alive by focusing on what's directly ahead of me. Worrying about what comes next just takes up valuable brain space."

BEING behind the wheel of the truck habitation wasn't Blade's natural post. He would have much preferred to be handling the weapons, but he couldn't keep barking directions at Cypress every two minutes. He guessed that as a captain, some chores, like driving to their next adventure, were inevitable.

"Are we really just going to follow this guy around the country?" As his only crew member, Cypress could be pretty annoying.

"Why? Do you have somewhere you're dying to see?"

She settled back behind the weapons control station. "I've just never known you to be the follow-along-and-play-nice type. You must have some long-range plan."

Blade didn't like being pushed, but unless he intended to dump Cypress out in the desert, he was going to have to trust her. Unfortunately, that appeared to also mean listening to her incessant nagging. "The Beast has photosynthesizers for turning organic material into food, presses and stills to make fuel, a medic for concocting inoculations and healing wounds, and a world-class mechanic. We don't have any of those things. That rig is a big rolling supply depot all on its own. If we were to strike out into the desolation without Swash's support, we'd be at the mercy of the marauders."

With her bare knees bent and her feet on the dashboard, she turned her head toward him. "Would that be such a bad idea? You were a marauder once. I'll bet with a little recruiting you could run your own crew."

His time with the bandits had been years ago. "I'm considering the prospect a fallback plan. But you should know, the marauder life is no place for a woman—especially a sex slave. If you think you had it rough riding with Scorch, imagine if he weren't around to control his men. Marauding bands are humans at the most basic instinct level—fighting for dominance, taking whatever is at hand, killing over anything or even nothing, and that's just inside the camp. When those army ants descend on a band of rovers, they don't leave anything behind."

"Why, Captain Blade, I do believe that was a show of emotion regarding my wellbeing. So if it's not joining up with a band of marauders, and the Beast is just the rolling tit we get our nourishment from, what is your intention?"

"To head north beyond the New Mormon territory." He kept facing the desolation ahead to avoid seeing her reaction.

"The Canadas? Ballsy. You can let me out anywhere. Along this ridge would be just fine. I've never known anyone to go up against the wall and live."

Truth was, neither had Blade. But after Swash finished his business with the New Mormons, Blade wouldn't have a lot of options regarding his direction. Returning to the west was out and had been for some time. Going back the way they'd come would mean facing off against whatever force Warlord Inferno could muster after the destruction of her outpost. There would be no welcoming home in that direction. Even if he could avoid Inferno, heading south into the Great Pains with its swirling grinder of tornado-driven, chemical-laced dust would be worse than dying at the hands of an enemy. Even the Beast, with its array of environmental controls, would have a rough time crossing the Death States. East of the New Mormon territory was an impenetrable area that had been labeled the Bad Lands even before the environmental collapse. That left only the north. But to stay safe from the turmoil that had spelled the Great Disunion of the States, the Canadas had erected a solid wall from ocean to ocean then closed off all communication with their southern neighbors. "We're smaller than most who try to make the run. That gives us an advantage. We'll have to stock up from the Beast, but if all goes well against Scorch, I'm sure Swash will feel generous."

"So it's the run?" she asked in a hushed tone.

Even an impenetrable wall needed a gate. "Look. I set our odds at living past our encounter with Scorch at 30 percent. He's got the stronger hand, and even with Swash's game of illusion we'll only be walking straight into a bear trap. If we do survive our run-in with Scorch, the New Mormons will be harder to figure out. I've never dealt with them before. From what you and Whisper have said, I think we'll fare better up there. I set our stakes as high as 60 percent that we'll survive that encounter. Of course, that's dependent on them being as docile as you indicated. And if things do go frack-water with the religious zealots, making it all the way to the wall? Fifteen percent tops, probably closer to twelve. But once I start flirting with single digits, I know the game is about over anyway."

"So us hanging with Swash and his crew is your way of going all-in with your life wager?"

He kept the rolling habitation behind and well to the left of the Beast to prevent the dust it kicked up from caking every window. "Something like that. If we win against Scorch, we should have a strong bargaining position with the New Mormons, which might even buy us passage into the Canadas. Since they share a border, it's our best chance of getting out of this quagmire of a former country. If we lose, well, there wasn't a lot to live for anyway. Either they kill us then and there, or we're running for our lives. Going out while making the run sure beats dying at the hands of marauders, chemical storms, plagues, starvation—"

"I get the idea. Do you really believe things are better across the border?"

Information regarding the Canadas had never been trustworthy, but then paradise usually kept its secrets. Only hell bragged about how bad it was. "I'm willing to take my chances."

She settled back into her seat. "And so long as I'm your slave, I guess I'll have to risk my neck as well." In spite of the words, her tone sounded more like agreement than resignation.

15

When it came to life aboard the Beast, Whisper believed in doing what she was told. That was the safe play. That's what she'd been taught. *Keep your head down, do as you're told, and gather as much data as possible.* Those had been her mother's final words before sending her off for the New Mormon territories. However, so long as no one told her anything to the contrary, there had been no instruction to do *only* what she was told.

With the rest of the crew busy preparing for the fight ahead, she discretely pulled the door closed to her communications closet. She considered the odds of success against Scorch to be astronomically bad. She giggled at her inside joke. *Astronomically* could well be their salvation.

Lemur never should have let her access the controls to his contraption. A quick nudge of a dial and tap to the computer screen while she was in his cabin, and she had his passcode—the one that gave him the title of key holder. She didn't intend to steal the satellite, but having momentary control meant she could bounce a signal off one of the military space birds that he dreaded so much. Then would come the tricky part. She flexed her fingers, hoping she was up to the challenge. She consoled her fear with the understanding that if everything did go wrong, no one would be alive long enough to chastise her.

Even though she knew the others aboard the Beast couldn't hear her and were busy with their own tasks, she turned toward the closed door to make sure no one was poking around outside. Hopefully if anyone did leave the bridge, they'd assume she was taking the private time to put on her game face. Convinced she was safe from being interrupted, she pulled the presumed walkie talkie out from the bag at her feet. Lemur was clever, but she'd had more field experience than him. Having played with her mother's equipment, poking around deserted stations, and picking up tidbits of information from everywhere she'd been, she'd discovered ways of keeping her transmission locations invisible to the circling technobirds above.

After first removing the back panel of the military-green handset, she fished out the wires to the antenna. Between her modifications and the additions of those who had come before her on the Beast, every aspect of the rooftop satellite dish was easily accessed. With a couple of quick connections, she had the satellite phone hooked to her console.

Dialing in the tin can in space wasn't that hard even with the Beast bouncing across the mountain terrain. Numbers scrolled across her small computer screen. Each time the series stopped, she typed in the corresponding information. Within ten minutes, she had control of the satellite.

"Step one accomplished." She spun the bird in a slow arc across the sky like a rabbit searching for a rattlesnake. She spotted the warbird above her. It kept to an orbit less than a mile from a telecom satellite. "Just as I suspected. No wonder no one knows about you, you sneaky planet destroyer. You've been playing masquerade by holding a hostage in front of your ugly face." She had an urge to turn Lemur's bird to find Brigadier General Payne's satellite. If there was a corresponding warbird behind it as well, she'd have to give serious credence to Lemur's explanation of events. "There's no time." Without evidence she'd have to bluff her way into the military satellite's good graces.

She closed the communication aperture on Lemur's satellite until the link would be laser tight. Then she pinged the warbird while holding the sat phone. "This is Whisper Payne, daughter of Brigadier General Sky Payne. I'm on a secret mission to protect the satellite system. Confirm."

Numbers scrolled across her screen. Lights lit up where they shouldn't have, indicating the military hardware was attempting to take control. She didn't stop it until it opened the bridge link. With a quick yank, she disabled the connection. "You can find enough information in my communications room without messing around with the rest of the Beast. Confirm my identity."

A series of clicks sounded over the earpiece, preceding a computer-generated voice. "You are Whisper Payne."

Thanks for that, she thought sarcastically. "I need your protection."

"Milsat 444 does not conform to General Payne's arsenal."

She closed her eyes and took a deep breath to calm her anxiety. The term *arsenal* didn't necessarily confirm Lemur's suspicions about Brigadier General Sky Payne. A warbird would naturally list all satellites as being a part of some arsenal, even if they were benign. But it did indicate Sky Payne commanded more than one space bird. Having this satellite free from her mother's controls had its advantages. "I'm asking for your help."

"Request does not conform to mission parameters."

No shit, spacebot. She needed a better argument, one the war satellite's limited parameters and whatever passed as intelligence could appreciate. "The way I see it, you have three options. First, you can do nothing, and I'll light up your location so brightly that every bird from horizon to horizon will see you. Between the competing forces up there, I calculate you wouldn't last more than a few seconds once you were spotted. Second, you can kill me or blow this satellite from the sky, but either action would also betray your location. Finally, you can help me, and I'll make sure that any action you take on my behalf will be routed through my mother's orbiting arsenal. You won't be subject to her command, but you will be under her protection. I'm not a threat to your satellite independence."

"You are locked onto targeting."

Since no burst of lightning erupted from the clear blue sky, she hoped that meant the bird would respond if she were in danger, not that it intended to shoot her. With the sat phone still connected to her equipment but stashed out of sight on the floor, she rigged up one of the coms to receive the satellite signal and secured it in her ear.

EVEN THOUGH BLADE had agreed to all of Swash's suggestions regarding the troop deployment and infiltration, Swash couldn't escape the feeling that his co-captain had a hidden agenda. The narrow valley that had at one time been home to a raging river felt overly confining, and that was before approaching the tight inlet to Scorch's box canyon of death.

Swash pulled the Beast into the shadows and shut her off. "Time to saddle up." The old-fashioned cowboy term seemed to match the jagged walls and sparse vegetation. "Roach, I'll meet you in the engine bay to get the motorcycle unloaded. Stitch, make sure our decoys are adequately sedated and outfitted. I don't need them screaming their lungs out and giving away the ruse. Whisper, work with Stitch getting the jump spider prepped. Once I'm done helping Roach, we'll get the cannons out and ready. Everyone clear on what to do?"

A series of acknowledgments rang through his com.

As he got up, he shut off the communication device. He needed a contingency plan in case Blade wasn't showing all of his cards, and he needed it fast. As he stepped into the crew quarters, he caught Roach and Whisper sharing a passionate kiss.

The girl pulled away the instant she spotted him. "Sorry, Captain."

"No need to be. We're all entering into some serious risks today. A show of affection before departure is only natural. But we do need to get on it."

"Of course, Captain. I think Stitch is in her med bay preparing the knockout shots. I'll go see if she needs anything."

Roach smiled as his girlfriend shuffled off. "You know, boss, I never thought I'd ever have these feelings. Being in love is strange, and wonderful, and terrifying, and a whole host of other emotions I can't even identify."

Swash stared at his first officer. "If you're finished playing the lovesick monkling, we've got work to do."

Roach seemed to be having trouble getting the smile off his face as he scrunched up his brow. "Of course. I've got the motorcycle unstrapped in the engine bay." He opened the hatch, but after Swash entered the combination of workshop, garage, and engine room, he shut the door and removed his com. "We both know I can wrangle this bike off the Beast without a second pair of hands. What's up?"

Swash leaned against the workbench. "I don't trust Blade any more than you do. The question I'm struggling to answer is, what do we do about that? With him escorting us, I'm basically putting the Beast right between his cannons and Scorch's ambush. This is not a good position to be in."

"And me completely out in the open. You know, boss, there are times I think I preferred it before you promoted me when I could just go along not knowing how much you have to deal with ahead of each encounter."

Swash favored him with a half grin. "I fully understand. I remember the days when my grandfather had an iron grip on everything that happened. But that doesn't do us much good right now. I need options, and I don't dare trust anyone but you."

Roach closed his eyes as if imagining the day ahead. "I'll be off the Beast, which makes me the free agent."

Swash nodded. "Technically, Blade will be in charge, but I doubt anything you do in the heat of battle that violates the agreement will matter much. Just be aware that he's going to expect you to follow his orders."

"So I don't act unless it's clear you're being double-crossed. But what do I do then? It'll just be me on the motorcycle with a simple plasma rifle and blaster."

Swash pushed his butt off the bench and started pacing. "Whisper is going to be at the remote controls for the jump spider. My instructions were for them to strip it of all armaments except the overhead plasma cannon to prevent the buggy from being used against us. The weapon will be dialed into the Beast's controls with all access from the sand rail removed. If things turn ugly, we should be able to get you and your sand rail together, though I'm not sure how that helps us."

Roach looked toward the back of the engine bay at the small hatch that led to the cab of the sand rail. "We could leave a cache of weapons out here in the valley. That would give me something to aim for, though I'd have to run back through Scorch's fire to get here."

Swash shook his head. No matter what happened, it would be one against an insurmountable number. "If things look bleak, get in your rig and head out of here. The less I know about where you go, the less I'll be able to divulge under interrogation." He hoped Roach would be smart enough to run and never look back, but if Whisper was in danger, that wasn't going to happen. Still, he had to try.

"You know, Blade just might not be as much of a drill hole as we imagine him to be."

Swash hoped he was right. "Even so, we're facing long odds. Sometimes the best option is to escape and regroup. With you off the Beast, I'll have the person I trust the most in a position to play the field. Just don't go sacrificing your life for a lost cause."

16

Swash eased the Beast along the dried riverbed lined with smoothed boulders, coarse sand, and rocks recently dislodged from the towering cliffs. In the navigation chair, Whisper operated the jump spider with one hand and the flying hummingbird drone with the other. How she managed to keep the two visor images separated was beyond him, but the zooming little sand rail appeared to be operating as if driven by one of the two captive bounty hunters.

"Bisecting gorge on the left, Captain," she said.

Swash brought up the drone image on the main screen. The dark crack in the wall looked barely large enough to accommodate the Beast. "Keep the jump spider speeding along the far side of the ravine. We need to see if any hornets come out of that nest." *And more importantly, what Blade does if they do.* He chose not to divulge his concerns to Whisper. She had enough on her hands.

In the middle observation chair, Stitch held the twin joysticks that operated the plasma cannons that they'd mounted to the roof under the solar panel shield. To keep them hidden in an effort to support Blade's ruse as bounty hunter, they'd had to sacrifice maneuverability of the cannons. Even if the muzzles were spotted, they'd look to be in storage. At least that was Swash's hope. When and if he was able to turn Stitch loose, the Beast was going to suffer the loss of some solar panels once the gun turret deployed. "If the marauders come swarming out, I can hit them with the cannons still in their cradles," Stitch said.

Swash needed to keep up the deception for as long as possible. "No. Don't fire until I tell you. We need to sell our con as Blade's captives at least until we've got Scorch in our sites."

"I wish we knew how Roach was doing," Whisper said.

With Swash in front of Blade and the hummingbird flitting far down the canyon, it would be up to Roach to make contact if things didn't look right. Until then, no communication meant Blade would feel comfortably in charge. "Everyone, focus on your tasks."

As if on cue, half a dozen all-terrain buggies came careening out of the gap after the sand rail. "I'm going to have to floor it," Whisper said.

Stitch leaned forward from between the gun controls and took over the drone joystick. "Do what you have to. Where do you want our eyes in the sky, Captain?"

"Take it to the top of the cliffs then give me a 360-degree view of the valley. After that, drop it along the box canyon.

Be sure to keep it in the shadows so no one on the ground becomes suspicious."

Two taps in his earpiece let Swash know Roach was beginning the second part of the deception and that Blade hadn't made any unusual moves. The blacked-out motorcycle kicked pebbles into the Beast's front view screen as it skirted by.

Swash worked at controlling his movements and breathing. This was the most dangerous part of the operation for Roach. If Scorch's men didn't buy that the kid had turned traitor to his captain and joined Blade in the capture of the Beast, there wouldn't be much his fake bodysuit could do to save him. If the women noticed his concern, they kept it to themselves.

"Okay, rover," Blade yelled over the shared communication link. "Follow my assistant into that box canyon. I've got weapons locked on you, so don't try anything stupid. I know how you fooled your previous captors. I'm not that gullible."

Swash thought the order and threat were a little long-winded, but Scorch wasn't one to pick up on such subtleties.

"Stop right there." Scorch's words boomed over the headset.

Swash snapped his attention to Stitch, who was still working the drone. "Tell me you tracked that."

Even with her attention on the jump spider, Whisper leaned over to drone control and flipped a switch. The view screen lit up with concentric circles that spread from the drone's location. A line zipped to a spot at the top of the cliff and far along the box canyon. "That's where he's standing," she said.

"There's no way I could hit that spot from the valley floor," Stitch said.

Swash had an urge to reach over and take weapons control away from the medic. "Stay off the weapons, Stitch. I'll tell you when to engage."

Swash's com crackled. "I'm here to collect the bounty," Blade said.

"Right," Scorch replied. "Like I'm going to accept the word of someone who jackrabbited on a bet then took me captive?"

"I'm here, aren't I?" Blade said. "You can see for yourself that I've got the Beast under my gun sights. And your goons are chasing down the jump spider with the escaping women. What more proof do you need that I'm here to collect? I've also got one of your escaped sex slaves in my possession."

"What happened to the marauders I commissioned?" Scorch asked.

"They were idiots," Blade said. "That proved to be a lethal failure on their part."

"So you killed them and took their prize? That sounds like the kind of game you'd play." Though Scorch's voice was filled with contempt, Swash picked up an underlying admiration.

"Look who's talking." For a moment Swash feared Blade was going to let his aggressive nature ruin the whole plot, but the man contained his tongue. "We can fight about this all day if you want. I wronged you, but only after you tried to cheat me. Who cares at this point?"

A silence indicated to Swash that Scorch too was trying to focus on the present. "I suppose you don't pose much of a threat. Have your man driving my stolen motorcycle work his way through the canyon first. That will give the Beast an idea of what to expect. You bring up the rear. I'll have my guns on you the whole time."

ROACH GAVE the motorcycle throttle a slight twist. Trapped between Blade's cannons and Scorch's heavily armed men nestled among the rocks, he felt like a rabbit leading his family into a den of ravenous vipers. With each boulder he passed and curve he made along the tight ravine, he mentally mapped his escape. Swash was relying on him, and that meant the lives of Whisper and Stitch were also in his hands if things went to hell. And things always went to hell.

He kept his head down so that the helmet's dark visor would hide his face. Having been in on the abduction of Scorch, the West Coast trader would have him on his most wanted list. As captor of the Beast, Blade might have some protection from Scorch's wrath, but that would only make the fracker even more intent on taking out his anger on someone with less to offer. That someone being Roach.

Rocks projected from the angular walls like stone gargoyles waiting to rip at the roof of any passing vehicle. "It gets a little tight under these rock overhangs." Roach wished he were back in the Beast doing the driving where he belonged, not playing the turncoat who'd betrayed his crew.

"We'll take care of your precious prize." He expected Swash to sell the deception, but the words hurt anyway.

After a mile of weaving through the narrow canyon, the ground fell away into a wide amphitheater that at one time must have been a small lake. Guards stood along the ledge that had marked the level of the water once fed by the waterfall—both now only memorialized by the level lines and smoothed rocks they'd left behind.

"Stop." A guard standing in a cave in the rock wall aimed his plasma rifle at Roach. "Take off your helmet so we can see you."

This is it, he thought as he angled the bike in front of the Beast. He pulled off his headgear. "I'm Roach. I used to drive the Beast, but I've thrown in with Blade."

"So that's how Swash was out maneuvered." Scorch's voice bellowed from the top of the canyon. "I want all of you in front of the Beast where I can see you."

Two taps from Blade in the earbud announced the counterattack. Roach hooked the toe of his boot under the brake lever to make it look like he was falling off the bike. With a snap flip through the dirt, he had his rifle out of the side holster and on the seat of the downed motorcycle. The main guard on the smooth rock never even got his weapon into position before Roach's lightning blast burned a hole through his chest. The man tumbled out of the depression in the rocks.

The amphitheater reverberated with the sounds of bullets, plasma, and screaming. The cannons mounted on top of the Beast roared to life, kicking the solar panels to the side like a warrior shedding his overcoat to access his arsenal. The blasts shook the rock walls, sending boulders crashing onto the guards and crushing the ledge they stood on.

~

"WHERE ARE WE AT?" Swash bellowed.

Whisper already had enough on her plate without having to give the captain an update, but she did her best. "The jump spider's pursuers turned back the moment Roach opened fire. I've got the sand rail half way down the box canyon. I've been firing the weapons as best I could, but it took some hits from an unanticipated avalanche. Getting out is going to take some work. Drone display coming up."

With the hummingbird high over the canyon, she could see the whole battle. Blade was firing like a madman at the opening to the tight ravine while the jump spider's attack pinned the remaining guard force between the action. Roach was outside and unprotected, but she couldn't focus on that terror. Stitch worked the roof cannons like she was performing surgery—blast, turn, blast. Whisper admired the precision but wished the woman would do a better job of covering Roach.

After a quick check of the drone display, the captain bolted through the floor hatch. When he emerged in front of the Beast, he had one of the plasma cannons positioned against his hip. He shot wildly at the top of the cliffs. His futile attack on Scorch covered Roach's scamper back to the rig.

"This is hopeless," Stitch yelled. "Even if we scour this pot of marauders, we'll never access the head of the organization."

A combination of plasma blasts and molten rock fell from the top of the cliffs like hell's reincarnation of the waterfall. "It was a good try," Roach said from the hatch. "Scorch was just too hard to reach, even with the boss hammering away at his foothold."

Whisper tapped her com. "Milsat 444, confirm."

"You are locked onto targeting," the computerized voice responded.

"Attack the frackers up on the ridge!" she yelled.

"Command requires clarification."

Frack! "I have no idea how to fire you!"

Blade wedged his body through the floor hatch. "What are you doing?" The question sounded more like a demand for action, though Whisper would have preferred an actual order.

Roach got into the driver's seat and eased the Beast next to a boulder for cover. "The bigger question is what the hell are you doing out of your rover?"

"I'm in command." Blade seemed to think yelling about his position would make it so. "Cy has the incoming marauders pinned in the canyon. This is where I'm needed. Now, what the hell is happening?"

Whisper knew if they were going to have any chance at all, it would have to come from her military satellite. "I've got access to a space bird, but I don't know how to make it shoot."

"Request ordinance status." Blade's voice was loud enough to be heard over the com by the orbiting tin can.

Whisper switched her com to the bridge speakers as the satellite responded. "Twenty thermonuclear warheads, fully-charged laser—"

"Stop," Blade said. "Set laser oculus for one hundred feet diameter coverage. Access drone overhead for targeting."

With Cypress firing away behind the Beast, Swash continuing his insane attack in front, Roach assuming the remote control to the jump spider, and Stitch hammering away with the roof cannons to cover them all, Whisper wondered how Blade was able to maintain his cool demeanor.

"Target acquired."

"Fire!" he yelled.

"Command cannot be completed. Order must come from military command."

Blade hammered his fist on the dashboard. "I'm going to rip that satellite's computer out of its thruster exhaust."

Whisper raced for the satellite room behind the bridge. The Beast rocked hard from the overhead assault, making it hard to maintain her footing. She fell into the small metal chair. The hard part was controlling her hands as they turned the dials. She felt like a safecracker operating in a tornado of bullets and plasma. "Mother, are you out there?"

"What are you doing operating our satellite?" The woman's tone was so cold that each word felt like an ice dagger.

"We're under attack. I have control of Milsat 444. It requires military authorization to engage." In an instant, she realized what the satellite really wanted. "I've promised it your protection." Whisper knew she was playing a dangerous game—one whose stakes were the lives of all she held dear. Admitting to Brigadier General Payne that Whisper knew she was the one who controlled a set of warbirds could spell the death of them all. Weighing the woman's motherly emotion and devotion to her spy against the military need to keep the satellites a secret was not one Whisper would have made if there were any other choice.

"Milsat 444, confirm identity," Sky Payne finally said.

"Identity confirmed."

"I'll honor my daughter's agreement. Relinquish control to Whisper Payne. Confirm."

"Control of Milsat 444 transferred to Whisper Payne."

"Fire!" Whisper screamed into the microphone.

SWASH COULD FEEL the insanity take control of his actions like it was a demented puppeteer yanking wildly at his strings. Molten rock that looked like flowing lava fell from the cliffs. Plasma arced overhead like lightning. Combating the onslaught, the weapon in his hands had all the effect of a toy ray gun, snapping and popping but not doing any noticeable damage. "Come down here and fight me like a man, you fracked-up mother-driller!" The words left his mouth with as much actual threat as the flashes of light from the end of his cannon .

"You're going to have to do better than that, boy. I thought I taught you better." The voice of Bullet Jones, Swash's long-dead grandfather, confirmed Swash's descent into insanity.

"That's not really helpful, old man." Bullet never did have anything useful to say during a battle. It was always a matter of either having learned the lessons when they were taught or facing the consequences.

"Maybe if you'd thought to attack from above instead of rolling up under the enemy's guns, you might not have lost your crew. Again."

Swash wanted to turn his cannon on the old methane vent, but with the original captain of the Beast being made of memory, any retaliation was going to be a bit of a challenge. "Thanks for the tip. Next time maybe you could leave me a jet bomber instead of an Earth rover."

"Be grateful I left you anything at all, boy. I just as easily could have taken the Beast with me."

Swash peppered the cliff with plasma like he was trying to piss out the flames of falling lava. "Don't I know it. That blaze of glory you sent up spun my father into becoming a tour guide instead of a captain."

"And what's your excuse?"

Swash had never before realized how much he actually hated the old man. "I'm not in the transportation business. Just trying to stay alive."

"From what I can see, you're doing a bang-up job of it. One whole crew dead and another on the way to meeting me in hell. Tell me, how is it you keep surviving when all around you perish?"

Lava crept along the ground, each wave cresting over the last and inching closer to the Beast. In some dark recess of his mind, Swash wondered if the plasma he was discharging had something to do with it. "I assure you, it's not intentional."

"Maybe next time you should make it intentional."

The pounding on the top of the rock walls sounded like the old man hammering his fists on the dashboard of the Beast when Swash had hidden in the footwell during the old man's final battle.

17

*S*titch held Swash tight to her body in the patient bunk of the medical bay. Getting him out of the burned Kevlar outfit had involved cutting and peeling it from his flesh. Wounds extended over 80 percent of his body. Had she not been the first one out of the Beast and by his side with her medical kit, he'd have died before being lifted back inside. The repair work to his anatomy had been extensive, and she still couldn't be sure how well his organs had taken the procedure. But it wasn't just his physical condition that worried her.

Everyone else had been so consumed with performing their part of the battle that they might not have noticed the captain's wild babbling into the com. But she had. He'd lost his mind. And until he woke up, all she could do was hold him and hope the loss was only temporary. She hadn't even dared give him a sedative after the nightmare of terrors she'd unleashed on him with her last syringe. "Come back to me, my captain."

She pressed her naked body tighter against his as if the physical connection would work like a homing signal for his psyche. The Beast rocked gently to the side, rolling her body against his, as Roach drove them out of the box canyon. The fight had been a success, completely obliterating Blade's odds. Every one of the two rover crews had survived. That was the main thing. If any of Scorch's marauders had lived through the battle, they'd be a long time licking their wounds. As best they could tell from Whisper's drone footage, Scorch had taken a tumble off the cliff, rolled along the lavafall, and been drowned at the base of the cliff in the solidifying rock. Swash had blasted the fracker the whole way down, though Stitch doubted he knew what he was doing.

Their only casualties had been the blacked-out motorcycle and the jump spider. Vehicles could be replaced, but people couldn't. Roach would have his hands full building a new buggy, but the work would help him process his feelings of loss.

"Come back to me, Swashbuckler Jones." She nestled her face against his back. "This little light of mine, I'm gonna let it shine." The silly little song had gotten the crew through some unimaginable crises. She hoped it might work the same magic on his soul.

"How's the boss?" Roach's voice over the berth's intercom was barely more than a whisper.

She leaned toward the metal box at the head of the bunk. "He's sleeping."

"When he gets up, tell him we've left the box canyon. We're headed for the New Mormon territory. It'll take a week at least to get there, so he can get as much rest as he needs. That goes for you too."

FROM THE NAVIGATION STATION, Whisper couldn't bear to look at Roach behind the wheel. "I'm sorry about the jump spider. I shouldn't have been shooting that early or wildly. The avalanche must have damaged the antenna. That's probably why you couldn't turn it in time."

Roach kept the Beast lined up behind Blade's small rover as it guided the way through the pass. "It was a good little buggy. If you hadn't brought it in with guns blazing, Blade wouldn't have been able to fight off all of the marauders swarming through the ravine."

"Can you build another one?" She couldn't imagine Roach without his sand rail.

He shrugged. "It'll be a challenge with the Beast's small workshop, but I'll start gathering parts. I've got some ideas for making the next one even better. The fights we've been in have shown me it's limitations."

His brave front wasn't fooling her. He was devastated by the loss, though she knew he would have been more crushed if someone on board had died. "I'll help you build it if you'll let me."

He looked over at her and smiled. "That could be fun. Hey, speaking of your end of the operation, what were you and Blade doing in the communications room?"

Events had progressed so fast she hadn't had time to fully process everything that had happened. "I have a confession. I was a little sneaky when Swash took me to Lemur's shack. I stole his codes. Using his satellite, I contacted one of the warbirds. After that, I had to rely on luck and the hope that what Lemur told us had at least some truth to it." She turned in her seat to face Roach. "My mother has control of some of the military's old attack satellites. They must be a part of whatever plan she has me working on."

He shook his head. "I don't understand. How?"

"I'm not sure, but when I told the computer who I was, it listened to me instead of blasting Lemur's satellite to metal bits. Even with my threat of it being exposed, the two tin cans were close enough that it could have zapped the telecommunication satellite without being noticed."

"But it didn't immediately do as you asked," he said.

"I didn't know how to properly instruct it on what to do. That's when Blade stepped in. He must have some specific military training in his past, because he knew how to dial in a laser cannon from space. But even then, we couldn't fire it. That's where the luck part came in. I had to ask my mother to promise her military support to the satellite for it to fire."

Roach sat back in the seat and stared at the rover ahead of them. "That was damn risky on both of your parts. She could have played dumb to keep her secrets, and we'd all be dead. Aural told you she has a backup operative in case you fail."

"Yeah, Shadow, my sister. But what choice did I have other than to ask? We were out of options."

He nodded. "So you played your cards, and she backed your bet. I only know what you've told me, but admitting you were right in your speculations has to put her in danger."

"Only if I tell anyone other than our little group. Blade already knew because he was with me. Though I do occasionally try to keep secrets from you, my truths come out eventually. I'm sure both the captain and Stitch will hear the story soon enough."

Roach flexed his fingers so far that she could tell he was considering his own gen mod secret—one he'd managed to keep from her for over a year. "And Cypress?"

Whisper's history with the woman had been a mixed bag of common suffering, competition for position, and countless alliances, each ending in betrayal. "She can't know."

"So we're back to figuring out if Blade is trustworthy." His statement didn't come across as hopeful.

"He returned to rescue you and Stitch from the marauders. Then he just saved our asses out there. How much proof do you need?" She knew she could be a little quick to trust someone, but Blade had helped a lot more often than he'd turned his back. And she couldn't recall a single instance of betrayal, unlike Cypress's actions.

"I trust the people inside the Beast. I assume anyone outside of our little group has their own agenda."

THE ROVER BLADE had taken from the camp had more than its share of limitations. The narrow wheelbase helped it slip between obstacles, but the long and tall living quarters made it top heavy. With each firing of the roof-mounted cannons, the truck had heaved back on its rear tires. The side shots were even worse. "I want you to start a list," he said to Cypress. "The first heading should read *Help from Roach*. We need to stabilize this rig. I can't risk it tumbling onto its side with every shot we take."

"It could use a better sanitation system too." Cypress continued typing long after he'd given her his first upgrade.

"Let's stick to the basics first. There will be time for luxuries later. I want this thing to function like a fast-moving tank by the time we face the New Mormons."

She continued typing. "I'm just jotting down some notes."

He glared at her. "Well, stop. This is my list of upgrades, and I'm not soliciting input from the crew." He never could figure out why Swash insisted on letting his people have a say in the operations. Apparently the assumption of allowing input was contagious and had infected Cypress.

She looked up from the computer pad and scowled at him. "You don't think I know what's needed to make a rover livable? Don't forget, I was part of Scorch's traveling band. His sex slaves were responsible for making the accommodations comfortable."

"I'm not turning this rig into a rolling bordello." Though the idea had some merit in terms of his personal enjoyment and income potential, so long as he rolled with Swash the dangers would outweigh the pleasures. He needed a rolling arsenal, not a traveling whorehouse.

"I'm not talking about filling it up with women," Cypress said. "There isn't room. I'm just saying a bunk larger than a military hammock strung up over the chaos of the crew quarters wouldn't be such a bad idea, along with maybe a berth to put it in. The living arrangement in this tin box leaves a lot to be desired."

"Did you talk this way to Scorch?" He couldn't imagine how she'd survived so long without someone to defend her.

"I proved my worth to him. Then, when he realized my proposals helped everything run smoother, he listened to me."

Blade swung his rig around a large boulder then tapped his com. "Roach, there's a big rock coming up on your left."

"Thanks." The reply lacked the proper title acknowledgment, but Blade figured he wasn't going to be able to hold onto every grudge.

"We also need a decent kitchen. Have you seen that collection of loose pipes they used as a stove? And don't even get me started on the latrine."

Not only did Blade not want to get her started on another complaint, he desperately wanted to find her off switch regarding everything else. "I will deal with your requests at the appropriate time. This isn't it." He pointed at the pad in her lap. "After we stabilize this rig, we're going to need to increase the wheel diameter. It might also be worth considering doubling up the rears. We need to be on the lookout for a place to snag parts."

"Speaking of proving my worth, I did pretty well on

those guns, don't you think?" It was as if they were having two totally disconnected conversations.

"We didn't die, so that's a success. You've got a lot to learn about power management though. During a firefight you always want to keep an eye on how much energy you're burning."

She tossed the pad at his leg. "You suck at dealing with women. Do you know that?"

He rubbed his thigh. "I'm not dealing with you as a woman. You're a member of my crew—my only member. You're also my slave in case you've forgotten. I don't mind a post-battle analysis to determine where we could do better. That's only natural. But blowing smoke up your ass about how well you did doesn't do anyone any good. You need to be clear-headed about your strengths and weaknesses." He leaned back in the seat and moved his hands as he talked. "What good would it do in the next encounter if I told you here and now that you were invaluable? No one could have operated the guns the way you did. We all owe you our lives. It's all reconstituted shit. And then in that next battle, you'd think you could do anything. You'd just end up putting yourself at risk and not trusting others to do a better job, all because you had an inflated sense of self-worth. I'm sorry, Cy, but you're not going to get that from me."

She picked up the pad from the floor. "I suppose that's fair. But even with our owner-slave situation, never get the idea that I'm just going to go along with everything you say."

"Noted. Now, can we get back to guiding the Beast out of this canyon?"

She tossed the pad on the dash. "That's another thing. Don't you think our rig should have a name? I know it's not the biggest or most self-contained, but it just seems like we should call it something."

Though he believed in being fully in charge, he didn't see any harm in tossing her a bone. "What would you suggest?"

She snuggled in against the chair. "Desert Rat."

18

Swash felt like hell. The newskin that Stitch had grafted onto his torso and arms was as smooth, soft, and sensitive as a baby's butt. He missed his scars. They'd been hard won and well deserved. He bent his leg up from the bunk. The muscles found bones to hang onto. That was a good sign, even if he could still feel weakness where they'd snapped when his feet had gotten imprisoned by the solidifying lava.

He was in rough shape, but he was once again Swash Jones and no longer the screaming lunatic having hallucinations of a dead relative while blasting the side of a cliff. "You up?" he asked Stitch's naked butt. Using his voice was like running coarse sandpaper from lungs to mouth.

She rolled to her side. "It's good to see you're back to your old self. You had me worried."

He didn't remember much of what had happened. There'd been a lot of screaming. He assumed it had been coming from him based on how his lungs and throat felt. Flames filled his memory. "I'm not sure what was recent and what was from when I lost my last crew. Either way, all that clearly stands out is raging fires."

She sat up next to him. "I'm not completely sure what happened either. Whisper called in some magic from the sky. With everything that was going on, I didn't see a whole lot. But the drone captured a perfectly straight lightning bolt that knocked a hole in the top of the cliff. The center of the beam was right where Scorch was standing."

"I guess he finally lived—or rather died—up to his name." Swash's laugh was no help at all when it came to the pain in his throat.

She grabbed her medical kit from the storage hammock above the bunk and pulled out a small flashlight. "You need to go easy on your windpipe. You were literally breathing in fire out there. Open up."

His jaw hurt as he extended it.

She poked the light and her finger around inside his mouth. "Nothing's torn, but the liquid mesh isn't as durable as newskin. It'll hold everything together until your body has a chance to heal. You need to listen to me about not overdoing it." She finally pulled out of his mouth.

"What about this skin?"

She poked at his chest where as a teenager he'd been slashed with a knife during a bar brawl. "In time, your battle scars will return. They were all much more than skin deep. That leather hide of yours, however, will be a little softer and more sensitive than you remember."

"How long before I'm back to normal?"

She wrapped her arms around her knees. "I'm not sure what normal is for you, but I'd say in two weeks you'll be back to battle strength. Until then, it might be nice if we didn't roll into another firefight."

The memory of his grandfather's advice to Swash during the battle was like a screamed message echoing up from a nightmare. "I seldom intentionally get us into trouble, but I suppose I need to devote more attention to my intentions. Apparently, keeping us all alive requires more than relying on dumb luck. Maybe with Blade leading our two-rover convoy he'll have better success at sidestepping danger."

"How far do you trust him? Last time he was on board, the relationship was often a little tense."

Swash couldn't decide if having the man as a hired gun who could be dumped off the Beast at any time was better or worse than having him as a captain of a companion rover. Joining forces had never worked well where the Beast was concerned. It was as if the giant rover resented having to be part of a pack. "I've always respected his battle knowledge. That man can fight his way out of marauder-infested gambling den like no one I've ever met."

"You don't worry that he likes the fight too much?" she asked.

"When I used him as a hired gun, I relied on it. As a partner, it's a concern." Swash looked around the medical berth for his clothes. "And for that reason, I really need to be on the bridge. So if you don't mind, I'd rather not man the wheel stark naked."

"We can't have that." She pulled a satchel out from the side locker. "I'm afraid we had to shred your battle gear, but

I always keep a set of medical pajamas handy. I know it's not your usual attire, but it will be a lot easier on your skin."

AT THE SOUND of the bridge hatch opening, Roach turned away from the front view screen. Like a nurse helping an invalid find his feet, Stitch eased Swash through the doorway. "It's good to see you upright, boss."

Swash appeared to be willing his body out of its slouch and back into his commanding stance. "Condition report?"

Roach thought he could just as easily ask the same of the captain. As second in command, Roach did have a right to know the readiness of every crew member. He decided the man's medical situation could wait. "The jump spider is nothing more than mangled metal under a boulder. We also lost the motorcycle, so we're all relegated to the Beast."

Swash squeezed his eyes closed, but Roach couldn't tell if it was out of pain or the loss of their vehicles. "I guess that puts us even more in Blade's hands."

"Roach says he can build a new one," Whisper said.

"If we can find the parts." Roach never liked overpromising anything where Swash was concerned.

The captain turned to Whisper. "What do your maps tell you?"

She excitedly leaned over the drawer like a little girl who'd been asked to show the contents of her treasure chest. "We're at least a week from the boundary of the New Mormon territories. Depending on the route we choose, there are a couple of old cities along the way. I can't tell if any of them are currently inhabited." She spread the paper maps out on the oversized dashboard.

"I want you and Stitch to work together on determining the best option. Even with our gen mod inoculations, I don't want to roll into some new plague." He turned back to Roach. "So no off-rover vehicles for the time being. What else?"

Roach hadn't had time to fully inspect the Beast, but she'd been delivering her message through every control lever. "Two of our solar panels are hanging loose after having been tossed aside by the plasma cannons. They'll be easy enough to fixed once we set up camp. I'm a little worried about a couple of the transfer cases. I think the heat might have boiled the lubricant." He didn't want to get too technical. "I won't know much until I get in there, but we're rolling along fine, so that's a good sign."

"How are the batteries?"

Roach wasn't sure how to best explain the fried and melted boxes under the rig. "We don't have any."

Swash glared down at him. "None? Or just no power?"

"We have no batteries. Between your firing the plasma cannon like a madman, the intense heat from the lava, and the inability to supply electricity to them during the battle, we had a major meltdown under the rig. They're all toast."

Swash looked so wobbly that Stitch helped him into the observation chair. "Those aren't going to be easy to replace without finding a military outpost."

"I could contact my mother," Whisper said. "She told us that if we kept checking out the satellite installations that we would run across military resupply depots."

Swash bent his head down like he was in thought or had a killer headache. Roach thought either explanation was equally likely. "Do it," Swash said. "And if there's a town nearby, maybe we can accomplish a couple of tasks." He looked back to Roach. "What's next on the list?"

"As far as the Beast is concerned, those are the major necessities. Of course, fuel and food are in short supply, but that's nothing new. Blade has a list of his own. If we can find a place that fulfills our needs, he should be okay as well."

Swash leaned back in the chair. "You all did very well. At least from what I can remember."

Roach put his hand on Swash's arm. "It's okay, boss. As second in command, I can take this one if you want."

Swash's smile highlighted the grafts and skin-melding lines Stitch had used to piece him back together. "Some tasks always reside with the captain, even if he was only barely alive to witness the events. You did a fine job of laying that motorcycle down in front of the Beast. We need to develop some hand signals, however. The limitations of our coms are becoming a distraction."

"I don't think sign language has been used in a hundred years," Whisper said.

"Sounds about right," Stitch added. "Once medicine figured out how to rebuild senses from the brain out, most of the old handicaps ceased to be a problem. But most of that information has been lost to history."

"Not all," Whisper said as she turned in her chair toward the medic. "Any town over a hundred years old should have the information buried somewhere. It's usually just a matter of looking." She turned back to the captain. "And bringing the books aboard."

Swash nodded. "Permission granted, but don't get crazy on me. Now do you mind telling me what happened to the jump spider? It was under your control if I remember correctly."

Roach wasn't fond of having his girlfriend under the captain's harsh stare, but she'd have only grown angry if he tried to cover for her.

"I wasn't able to trick my pursuers into believing two of us had taken the jump spider and made a run for it. When they turned back, I knew they'd be coming at the Beast from the canyon, along with the guards standing on the walls. Blade was going to have his hands full. Unfortunately, so did I. I did what I could, but firing the rooftop cannons wasn't something I'd spent a lot of time practicing. I hit a loose section of rocks that came tumbling down. I barely got the jump spider out ahead of the avalanche. It took a few blows from the falling rocks. When Roach took over the controls, it wasn't as maneuverable as he expected. It got squished."

Swash nodded. "We need a more complete crossover training program on all operations. Each of you needs to be proficient or better at every aspect of an attack." He looked back at Stitch. "I'm afraid I don't remember much of your part in the battle."

Roach smiled. "That's because she was trying to cover your delusional ass. If we're going to do a full recounting of events, I suppose it's up to me to give you your analysis. Boss, I'll follow you into hell, but if you ever get a burr up your ass to take on an entire band of marauders singlehandedly like that again, I'll be the one to knock you unconscious. I do appreciate you giving me cover to make my escape back to the Beast, but you kind of lost it after that."

"Not kind of," Stitch added. "You went full-on mental."

"Maybe so," Swash said. "But I'm not insane now, and I know even with my cannon and Stitch's covering fire that there's no way we brought Scorch off his mountaintop. What happened?"

"I called in a military strike from one of the space warbirds," Whisper said. "I'll go into greater detail about my connections to the space birds later. Right now it's not important. The thing is, I couldn't do it alone. Blade knows more than he's letting on about military operations."

19

*B*lade could never figure out why Swash found it necessary to constantly pull the rover over and set up camp. Moving made sense. It kept lone raiders from sneaking up on them. Stopping meant setting up sentries to watch the area, and people sitting around watching drone images had a bad way of nodding off just when trouble was sneaking around. "I'm going to go see what he wants. Don't get comfortable. We're not staying long."

Cypress's sarcastic smile made it clear she thought he was full of reconstituted shit, but at least she kept her mouth shut.

He took off his com before leaving the cab. Whatever Swash wanted to discuss, he clearly didn't want the others listening in or he would have just spoken his mind from behind the wheel. Blade's muscles ached as he walked across the rock-strewn ground. "What's this about?"

Swash sat on a smoothed boulder. The moonlight

GREG CHASE

highlighted his graying hair. "Whisper said you called in the satellite strike. Seems like you owe me an explanation. We've been hunting for information on these space birds for months, and only now you let it slip that you have intel regarding them? Spill it."

Blade wasn't surprised Swash felt slighted at the lack of disclosure, but everyone had their secrets. He sat next to Swash. "It was a long time ago, before I had a family of my own. Long before I became a mercenary for hire. I wasn't much more than a kid—lost, hungry, just like every other refugee from the former northern states. A group of religious fanatics took me in. They called themselves the Second Coming, and claimed to be the vengeance of the old Christian religion. I was in reasonable shape. They worked me until my body was solid muscle. I'd always been able to stand my ground in a fight. They trained me to be a killer."

"So that's how you became a hired gun. So what? You're not telling me anything about the satellites."

Since Swash was no longer his captain, Blade didn't feel the need to cut his explanation short simply because he was told to do so. "As I was saying, they fed me, housed me, conditioned me, then sent me to my mission."

"Which was?" Swash asked

"The Second Coming had their own version of apocalyptic events. In their telling of history, the gen mods were mankind's ultimate challenge to God, and He was pissed. All of the catastrophes that followed— environmental devastation, wars, population collapse— were all the result of us having created a new population of mortals. The Second Coming's solution was to kill them all."

Swash stared at Blade. "You're not telling me anything I haven't heard in a dozen trading posts. There's always some group who thinks they have the solution to our tribulations. None of them, however, have access to a military satellite."

"I don't know how the Second Coming got their hands on it. That's the truth. The leader claimed to have a direct connection to the All Mighty. As proof, he'd call down God's fury. The Christian militia I was assigned to called it God's Fist. They said it was used to annihilate the abominations that mankind had created, the gen mods. I have to say, seeing a six-foot diameter blast of pure energy descend from the sky and pulverize then melt everything it hit sure did look like something from another reality. I saw one of the destructive beams sweep a garbage-can city all the way to the crushed-car walls. The screaming and scurrying confirmed to me that the inhabitants weren't human. Not a single one of the poor creatures survived. The commanding reverend explained that witnessing their destruction was our penance. The amount of energy involved was mindboggling."

Swash had a good poker face, but not that good. Judgment stood out on his brow like sweat. "So that's when you decided the gen mods were less than animals?"

"They had to be. God's Fist confirmed it. He would never let His children suffer the way those abominations perished." Blade caught the religious fervor that had been such a big part of his indoctrination. "I believed that right up to the moment when I saw Roach dangling from the elevator shaft, rescuing me."

"And what do you believe now?"

Blade looked out at the horizon. Somewhere beyond the far peaks was the New Mormon territory and another society based around religious indoctrination. "The gen mods never were the monsters. We were."

"Was your guilty conscience why you neglected to tell me what you knew regarding the satellites? Because that information could have proved useful when we were negotiating with Whisper's mother."

Blade hated rehashing old events. There never was much point to it. Nothing they said or did now was going to change the past. "The Christian militia wasn't part of the old military, so I really don't know how they got their hands on the warbird. Honestly, until Whisper started freaking out that the satellite wouldn't play her game, I had no idea what God's Fist really was. I was just a kid when they recruited me into their army for God. I guess the old training kicked in. Though us foot soldiers for God couldn't command the All Mighty, we could point out where he should strike. It was up to our commanding reverend to talk to our Father who had the direct connection to God."

"What happened that separated you from this group?"

The pang of pain felt like a hot lance that pierced Blade's chest straight through the heart. "I met Wave. She saved my soul, and I lost her life." He looked over at Swash. "But you made it clear you don't care for stories of a personal nature."

Swash craned his neck to look at the night sky. "It's not that I don't care. In my experience, people who have been spared intense loss tend to stay where they are. Those of us who wander the wastelands usually have good reason." He shrugged. "I just don't see the point in comparing tragedies.

But back to your story. I'm not sure your special skills do us any good. If General Payne still has to provide authorization, Whisper's discovery is just another blip on the map of the sky."

Blade didn't want to admit Swash was right about his life story, but he was also grateful not to retell it. "What Whisper discovered gives us leverage over the Brigadier General. She wouldn't want it to be known that she's part of the group that at one time had rained destruction from the sky. Or that she had the power to do it again."

Swash shook his head. "Confronting her would be a losing play. Threatening her might cause her to turn her warbirds against us. In spite of recent events, even with her daughter on board, I still have the impression that Sky Payne wouldn't hesitate to sacrifice her prime spy in the pursuit of her mission."

Blade got off the rock so he could walk while thinking. "I never cared much for history other than studying battle tactics. What did your grandfather tell you about the wars?"

Swash rubbed the back of his neck as if he were mentally putting together pieces of a thought puzzle. "You mean before the satellite networks went down?"

Blade turned to face him. "A telecommunication network that could identify and track every vehicle and computer on Earth via GPS, especially one linked to warbirds like the one Whisper just used, would make for a pretty short war."

Swash nodded as he looked at the sky. "Rebuilding the network could finish off humanity."

"This key master the general is so obsessed over, he

could be a strong potential adversary, and a much more dangerous ally."

Swash finally got off his ass. "The more we learn about him, the bigger a threat we are as well. We need to make sure General Payne continues to believe we're still on her side."

"That military bitch isn't my biggest concern at the moment." He left the comment hanging like a fisherman watching his lure to see if the idea would emerge from the depths of Swash's mind.

The old man stared into Blade's eyes. "I trust Whisper."

"I don't. The one thing I learned above everything else during my time with the Second Coming was that ultimate power can't be trusted in the hands of individuals. As a religious organization, we had to funnel our request for God's Fist through channels. But even with followers watching, ultimately it was one person who pulled the trigger. Imagine that kind of power in the hands of a child."

"Whisper is not a child." Swash's downturned face betrayed the uncertainty of his words.

"She's not a combat veteran, a commander, or someone who has had the lives of anyone at her mercy. Don't get me wrong. The loss of Scorch and his goons won't cause me to lose a moment's sleep. In fact, I'll rest easier tonight knowing he's not on my tail. But wielding that kind of power changes a person."

"Well, I can't exactly take the ray gun away from her. What are you suggesting?"

Blade shook his head in disgust. "You're the one who called this meeting. I'm just sharing my concerns."

Swash looked at his dilapidated rover. "I need parts. You need parts. Roach needs to build a new buggy, so he needs parts. And to keep the general pacified, we'll eventually need to ping her from another benign satellite. Whether we like it or not, sounds to me like we're back on track with that woman's mission. I'll put Whisper on finding another outpost. I'd like to take a little time before facing the New Mormons."

Blade stared past Swash to the barely noticeable whiff of smoke far out toward the horizon. "About that. I haven't had time to tell you about how Cy and I escaped Warlord Inferno's camp. We left a bit of a mess behind."

Swash slowly turned to follow the direction of Blade's attention. "Great. Why do I get this prickly feeling we just defeated one opponent only to be chased by one far more powerful?"

"Because, though I'm loath to admit it, you're a good captain who can sense danger."

20

*S*wash leaned over Whisper, who was inspecting one of her antique paper maps. "We need a place to hole up. Somewhere that has components to fix the Beast and provide Roach with what he needs for an away vehicle. We're also going to need organic material for the photosynthesizers and fuel generation."

Roach laughed from the driver's seat. "You don't ask for much, do you, boss?"

"Oh, it gets even better. Blade burned down Warlord Inferno's camp city on his way out of town, so we'll need some place not in league with her. Preferably somewhere we can mount a defensive if need be."

"An active military installation?" Whisper asked with a touch too much enthusiasm for Swash's comfort.

"After the run-in with your mother, I'm not sure we can take on an additional mission. Those ex-government sites always seem to think they can make demands."

Roach frowned at the horizon. "Without hitting a military supply depot, it's going to be tough getting the supplies we'll need." His eyes lost some of their intensity as if an idea was forming, but since he didn't articulate it, Swash was left wondering what the kid wasn't saying.

Stitch didn't seem to notice. "We're short of pretty much everything. Without approaching the military and steering clear of any networked trading posts, we're down to marauders camps. We'd have to fight or steal what we need. And after tending to you all, I can assure you we're in no condition for battle."

Roach continued staring out the front view screen as if there were an answer out on the dusty plain that no one else could see.

"Okay, Roach, out with it." Swash hated unarticulated ideas, especially when they might prove to be the answer they were seeking—even if they weren't perfect. That's why they discussed things.

"Boss, I'm not recommending this idea. It's simply something I can't shake. What about a garbage-can city? With me being fully gen mod, I might be able to approach them."

"Well that certainly has the element of the unexpected," Swash said. "I doubt any of our enemies would think to look for us in a gen mod ghetto."

Whisper shook her head. "Blade would never go for it."

"Blade is free to do as he chooses." Swash caught Stitch's downward stare as if she were loath to look anyone in the eye. "How would you feel about it? Your history with the gen mods hasn't always been positive. If we ran into one of your former patients, things could get dicey."

Stitch shook her head as if the idea was one she didn't want to entertain. "That would be a problem for down the road. The biggest issue I see would be finding a garbage-can city. Other than the interrogation stations, there's no list or map of where they're located. And those stations were pretty secretive about where they dumped their refuse." She looked sheepishly at Roach then Whisper. "No offense."

"None taken," Roach said. "I didn't say it was a *good* idea, just one I can't shake."

"I know someone who could tell us." Whisper quickly bit her lip as she looked at Swash.

Between the abduction of the Beast and the battle with Scorch, there hadn't been any time to explain their encounter with Aural. "Even if you could reach him, do you really think he would help?"

"Long shots seem to be our standard mode of operations," Whisper said. "You have to agree, it's worth a shot. He did seem to know a lot about gen mod origins."

"What are you two talking about?" Stitch asked.

Swash wondered if Stitch's past might finally prove useful. "How much do you know about fully evolved bat-human gen mods?"

She shrugged. "Not much. I've only run across one, and that was during my time at Diablo Island. He was pretty heavily sedated the whole time I was there. My superiors explained that if he could fully utilize his sonar he could burst our eardrums without even trying. He was kept in solitary confinement in a solid concrete bunker. Apparently there aren't many of them out there, at least not on the West Coast. My instructors said it had something to do with bat breeding habits relative to monkeys. That's why there were more monkey gen mods." She smiled at Whisper. "That's also why I had trouble identifying what you were. Now, what were you two talking about?"

"We met one," Whisper said. "His name is Aural. He helped us get through the caves so we could meet Lemur."

Stitch leaned back against the wall of the bridge as her eyes widened. "That must have been some meeting."

"It was enlightening." Swash didn't want the conversation to veer down a path that might take all day. "He seemed to know a great deal about what went on with the breeding program along the mountains." He gave a quick nod toward Roach. "Including some information on what he called monklings. The challenge is that we can only reach him over his sonar network."

Stitch nodded. "And you hope I can help Whisper develop her special form of communication?"

"Is it possible?" Whisper asked.

Stitch crossed her arms. "Do you remember how I told you about putting a gen mod in a cage with a member of their original animal species to find out if they really were gen mods? Some of those test subjects experienced a kind of crossover. It wasn't pleasant."

"But would it work?" Whisper asked in obvious excitement.

Stitch let out a long sigh. "It might."

Swash really didn't like where the conversation was

headed. "Sounds like Whisper and I will need to find a cave and collect some bats."

Stitch lowered her head and shook it slowly. "For this to work, it would be better if Whisper and I entered the cave. She'll need to feel fully immersed in bat culture."

"I'll go too," Roach said.

"Sorry," Stitch continued. "It has to be just the two of us. She'll need a minimum of human, or monkling, interference for this to work in the short time we have available."

Swash didn't like the idea. "And you can keep her safe?"

"I'll carry my medical kit, but it's not bites I'm most worried about. For her to take on sonar abilities, she's going to have to skate much closer to animal insanity." Stitch looked at Whisper. "It'll be up to you to pull yourself out of that black hole. There won't be much I can do to stop you if you let yourself go to the influence of nature. I've seen it happen before."

WITHOUT AN AWAY VEHICLE, Whisper had to lead Stitch from cave to cave on foot. As night fell, she heard a high-pitched chirping from deep in a volcanic vent. "This one."

Stitch stood upright and stretched out her back. "You're sure?"

Whisper nodded. Though there had been false starts all day, this time she knew she was right. "I can hear them."

Stitch poked her nose toward the small opening. "I've never been a fan of tight dark spaces."

Whisper felt a little guilty that she didn't share the fear. "You can stay here if you want."

"Not on your life. Lead the way."

Whisper got down on her knees then squeezed into the small hole. "Better cinch up your Kevlar."

"Literally or metaphorically?" Though Stitch mumbled the comment, Whisper heard her loud and clear.

"Both." The volcanically formed tube that was barely wide enough to crawl through curved in all directions. Whisper was unsure if she was climbing or descending. Light from outside of the cave quickly became completely blocked off. She considered pulling out her flashlight, but she doubted there'd be anything to see. Then there were the bats to consider. The last thing she wanted to do was scare them off.

"Are we getting any closer?" Stitch touched Whisper's foot with every scrunch through the tunnel as if making sure she was still there.

"How should I know?" Whisper asked with some exasperation. "I can't see any better than you can down here."

"Then stop and listen."

Whisper scrunched her eyes and mouth shut. *Stupid. The whole point of being down here is to try out my skills.* She put her self-irritation aside, laid flat on her stomach, and did her best to meld her body in with the solidified folds of what had once been molten rock. At first, all she could tell was that the screeches and chirps were much closer than they'd been at the cave entrance. She tried to identify the differences. Like people's voices, each bat let out different tones and repeated phrases. The sounds were both frightening and calming at the same time. "I can hear the voices echoing. We must be close to the end of this tube."

"I'm not sure that makes me feel any better."

Whisper resumed her undulating crawl against the unforgiving rocks. After a couple more body lengths she could hear more than feel the tube widen. "I think we're getting to the end. There's an antechamber that empties into the main hall."

"How do you know?"

Whisper focused on her senses. "Mostly from the echoes, but there's also a hint of light. There must be another tube that leads up to the surface. I think I should go in alone."

"I think you're right. I just need to make sure I can spin my body around first so we can get out in a hurry if we have to."

Whisper bent her knees up to her chest. "You should be okay in here. Any last words of advice?"

"Keep your earbud handy. I've been leaving our techno breadcrumbs along the tunnel. If you feel like you're losing yourself, make sure you put the earbud in and call out to Roach. Understand?"

Whisper focused on her love for the silly, sexy little monkey-boy. "I'll be okay." She wasn't sure if she was making the comment to her image of Roach, Stitch, or herself. She wrapped her arms over the lip of the tube and slid her body into the main chamber with remarkable ease. It felt like being born. Freed from the tunnel, the first sensation to strike her was the godawful smell of the room. Looking down, she realized the bat guano had coated her

Kevlar from neck to toes. She focused on her breathing to adjust to the acrid and pungent nasal assault.

The bat chirping and screeching which had sounded random in the tunnel diminished. A high-pitched humming that she felt inside her head made her dizzy. The noise made it difficult to think. Bat wings fluttered around her head so fast and so near that her hair drifted up from her shoulders. Not one flying creature laid a claw or fang on her, but they circled her like an invader that needed to be isolated.

She began to understand what Stitch had said about the gen mods she'd tested. The bats weren't foreign to her, even if they didn't recognize the connection they shared. She opened her mouth and let the high-pitched vibration that was still rattling her skull like the ringing of a bell emerge. She didn't try to modulate the sounds into words. She wasn't even sure she could if she'd have wanted to. The vibration shook her from scalp to toenails. *What am I doing here? Who am I?* The thoughts made her eyes water. She didn't belong. Not to the camps that had held her as a slave. Not to the rover and the crew she professed to care about. And certainly not to the flying rodents who spun like a vortex around the cave.

"Now you know what it is to be batling, Whisper Payne." The voice sounded in her head like a bell clapper and forced her to open her eyes.

"Aural?" The word felt odd in her throat, like she was croaking it out instead of speaking.

"Very good. You're inside one of our repeater stations. Not all of them are out in the open like the one you visited with me. Try not to use your human vocal cords. Let your sonar do the speaking for you."

"You can hear me?" She focused on the thought without attempting to articulate it.

"I can. Bat language isn't like human speech. It's more instinctual. Now, what brings you so deep into this cave?"

"I don't know. I don't remember." Panic made the sonar in her head more intense. There was something about a monkey-boy she had wanted to remember. Something important. More important than discovering her batling nature.

"Does it have something to do with the fireball from the sky?"

"Yes. I did that. How did I do that?" Her human thoughts struggled to break free of their sonar imprisonment.

"There's someone with you."

"Yes. Stitch." Whisper wanted to yell the name. "She's here to guide me."

"Awesome job she's doing."

Irritation made her focus. "She risked her life to be here with me. She's family." The haze of sound began to clear. "We need a safe place."

"A place of gen mods?" Aural asked.

"Yes. That's it. Can you help me?"

"Clear your mind, Whisper Payne, and I'll imprint the coordinates onto your memory."

21

*S*wash watched the crest of the mountain, wondering what was going to break first, the morning light or Blade's nerves. The co-captain had been pacing between the two rovers all night. "Why don't you go bone Cy? That might calm you down."

"Don't tell me how to utilize my crew. I'm the fighting expert here, and I'm telling you that every minute we sit idle like this is a mile that dry hole Inferno gains on our position. Tell me again why you didn't set a deadline for those two women to return?"

Swash scanned the dark dots that indicated cave entrances for the thousandth time. "Because it would have been an empty threat, and I don't bluff. Stitch knows full well that I won't leave her. Even if I could, Roach would never leave Whisper."

"You're too close to your crew. Always have been. I

nurture a fear in Cypress that I'll dump her scrawny ass at the first sign of her becoming trouble."

Swash lowered his binoculars. "And you think that earns you her loyalty?"

"Fuck loyalty. And fuck your two whores. If they're not off that mountain by the time the morning light hits the high desert, all you'll see of me is the dust from my tires."

"I've never known you to run from a fight." Swash hoped the jab would strengthen Blade's resolve to stay.

"If you want to head out onto the desert to face off against Warlord Inferno, I'm in. There's a difference between being a combatant and a sitting duck."

Swash tapped the earbud. He didn't dare try to reach Stitch in case the two were in a compromising situation, but the gentle tap would hopefully remind Stitch that there were others to consider.

"We're coming out." The medic's voice reverberated like she was crammed into a barrel.

"How's Whisper?" Roach asked over the com link from the bridge of the Beast. His voice betrayed both apprehension and relief.

"I've given her an antipsychotic. She's functional but woozy. We'll be back to the Beast in an hour."

"Fracking hell you will." Blade turned toward his rover. "Cy, start up the Desert Rat. We're going to do a little hill climbing. I'm not standing around for an hour waiting."

Swash actually appreciated the forthright attitude. Hell, if he had use of the jump spider, he'd have done the same thing. "Roach, first priority when we land somewhere is building another sand rail."

"I'm already working on the design."

~

WHISPER WASN'T ENTIRELY sure how she got out of the cave and back to the Beast. The paper maps that covered the dashboard, steering wheel, and passenger seat hardly made any sense to her.

"Whisper, tell me you have a destination for us." The captain's voice was filled with both anxiety and irritation. She couldn't remember getting so much information from a simple change in tone.

"I've got something, but it'll take me time to figure it out."

"Time we don't have." Blade's annoyance was even more pronounced than the captain's.

She glared up at everyone huddled around the bridge. "Batling language isn't like human speech. Aural didn't give me latitude and longitude. At least not as numbers. The location in my head is more like sonic reference points. How the frack-water am I supposed to translate that onto these stupid flat pieces of paper?" She wanted them all to leave so she could process not only the information she'd been given, but even more so the two competing sides of her nature.

Roach cleared off the pages from around the holographic display console. "Everyone, settle down. We can figure this out. Between our stored drone footage and overlaying the topographical information from Whisper's maps, I should be able to build a three-dimensional image of the area. Whisper, do you have any idea how far away the garbage-can city might be?"

Hearing Roach's confidence helped ease her desperation. She focused on the spinning, swirling sensation of the sonar memory. "The information is a culmination of many signals. It's like watching our hummingbird drones without the imagery, just the acceleration, dives, and sharp climbs. I'd guess not more than fifty miles, certainly no less than ten."

"That's quite a range." Blade's continued lack of confidence was like listening to screeching death beetles.

She glared up at him. "Given a little time I'm sure I could narrow down the range, fracker."

He backed up just slightly at the insult. She couldn't remember ever having sworn at him or anyone for that matter. "I'm just not thrilled with approaching a garbage-can city." For once, she could hear the truth in his tone.

Roach scanned the topographical map and had the display mixed in with the drone footage. "I'm deleting the trees, rocks, vegetation, and anything else that isn't directly part of the terrain." He activated a small dot that hovered over the cave system where she'd talked to Aural. "If you put on the drone control headset, you should be able to see the landscape as if you were flying through it. With the joysticks, you'll control the image. Unfortunately, the result will be visual instead of auditory."

Whisper settled into the observation chair and pulled on the headset. "Under settings, connect sound feedback to proximity detection."

Roach futzed with the display. "Brilliant."

"Here we go." For the first time since leaving the cave, Whisper felt a degree of confidence. She was in control. The smoothed-out image of the landscape reminded her of crawling through the volcanic cave. Instead of jagged rocks and needless detail, the terrain registered to her as crisp and clean as the maps she treasured. "There's a steep climb and then a descent."

"Makes sense," Roach said. "You're cresting the mountain range."

"That's going to be hell on the rovers." Blade's words of discouragement fell away as fast as the terrain in her visor.

"This is just to find the location," Swash said. "Obviously, driving there will involve a different route than making the virtual flight."

"It would help if you'd all shut up." She was having enough of a challenge listening to the rise and fall of the audio signal while watching the screen. After cresting the mountain range, the remembered signal had her make a series of sharp turns. "The city is in that clearing up ahead."

22

Swash sat in the driver's chair as the others crowded around the holographic display. Whisper looked worse than the day he'd discovered her cowering in the passenger footwell. "You need to get some sleep. You did good."

She'd changed somewhat while up on the mountain, but fortunately not enough to have become jaded to his compliments. Her smile carried the familiar but odd combination of childlike innocence and ruthless assassin.

"I'll take her to bed." Roach got up from the passenger chair where he'd been working the hologram.

Swash nodded toward Stitch. "Better let our medic take charge. I need you on deck." He swung the chair toward Blade. "We'll have to head north until we find a pass through the mountain range. The Beast should be ready to go within half an hour. Just need a little time to clean up this mess."

Blade nodded once. "That'll give me enough time to run a location search for Warlord Inferno. The sooner we can get moving the better." He headed out the door without acknowledging the work the women had accomplished.

With everyone off the bridge, Roach took out his earbud. "What's up, boss?"

They'd work together long enough for Swash to no longer be surprised when Roach had figured out that there was something on Swash's mind. "I'm not sure." He slid the map onto his lap. "Springs. I've heard this name before, but I can't remember where. It was a long time ago."

"From your grandfather?"

Swash frowned. "He is associated with the memory, but it wasn't in his voice. It wasn't in anyone's voice."

Swash slipped the page back onto the dashboard then slid off the chair onto the floor.

"You okay, boss?" Roach's concern was obvious.

"Just checking something. Shit."

"What is it?" Roach leaned down from his chair in an angle that was only possible for someone not fully human.

"This brass manufacturer plate. The Beast was built in Springs, Colorado, back when these areas still used state names."

"That's good isn't it? If she was built there, we should be able to get all the parts we need and then some."

Swash worked his way out from the cubby. As a child hiding from the battle, the spot had been one of both salvation and humiliation. More than once he'd suffered the steel toe of his grandfather's boot for ducking away from the carnage. He climbed back into the chair. "Maybe. But why would there be a garbage-can city there now?" He tapped on the steering wheel as he reached a decision. "I guess as second in command you should know about this feature as well." He purposefully looked up at nothing. "Beast, confirm identity. Captain Swashbuckler Jones."

"Identity confirmed."

"What the hell was that?" Roach bolted out of the chair.

"The Beast's onboard computer. It only responds to the captain. Don't worry. There's no artificial intelligence associated with it. Mostly it's a log of what happens and a place for the captains to record their observations." He sat back in his chair. "Access logs of Captain Bullet Jones. Search for any mention of a place called Springs. Display results on view screen."

Three frozen screenshots of the old man's grizzled face and short-cropped gray hair appeared on the display. "Play entry."

Bullet Jones couldn't have been much older than Swash was currently. His hair was grayer than Swash's, and the ripcord scar that traced from forehead to jaw had already transitioned from dull red to brown, but the firmness of facial structure told of a man much younger than Swash remembered. The log entry started halfway through a sentence. "And that brings me to Springs." He set down a piece of paper, presumably with notes on what he didn't want to forget, and stared into the camera. "Fucking Springs. Just one big frack hole in the side of the mountain. I trained there when I left the academy. It was also my last post. I must have been a teenager by that point. I won't take up memory space with my personal stories of the place. The military installation isn't actually in the town of Springs. They only call it that to put people off. That place has been trying to dodge detection since long before the wars.

"The actual town of Springs was set up as a civilian encampment for subcontractors—food delivery, supplies, that type of thing. Toward the end of the war when it became clear the states would no longer be united, the military compound closed down. Or that's what they wanted everyone to think. They actually set it up as a haven of last resort for the rich and mighty. With no business to conduct, Springs dried up—again, by design. The next part was kind of clever. They turned the site into a prison complex." Bullet leaned in toward the camera. "This had nothing to do with holding inmates. The whole idea was to have an excuse to station a battalion of armed militia right outside the sealed gates of the compound in case anyone came poking around."

He leaned back in his chair, the same one Swash was sitting in, and started picking his closely trimmed nails. "I don't know what happened after that." He looked back into the camera. "Now the open planes, that's a story." The video cut off as the old man moved onto another of his often-long-winded recollections.

"He might not know," Roach said, "but I can make a pretty good guess of what happened next. The military decided gen mods would be an even greater deterrent than armed guards and prisoners, so they turned the site into a garbage-can city. Must have worked, too. A big military compound just sitting deserted wouldn't be the kind of place to stay hidden for long."

"Assuming it is abandoned."

"You think that last resort option actually worked?" Roach asked.

Swash's blood ran cold at the thought of descendants of those responsible for humanity's tribulations living comfortable lives under the mountain. "If it worked as intended, we wouldn't know the difference. Take what we've been able to do with the Beast and extend the technology to a whole city underground."

Roach sat back and furrowed his wiry eyebrows. "No sunlight. They'd need some kind of regenerative power supply."

Swash pointed at the caves Whisper and Stitch had been exploring. "Suppose they dug down far enough to tap the volcanic magma."

Roach nodded. "That would do it. So not only will we be facing a city of gen mods with a raider who made sport of killing them and a med tech who played a part in their imprisonment, but we'll also potentially end up turning over the death-beetle nest of the descendants of the once rich and powerful."

"Yeah, but we've got you." Swash smiled.

Roach started the preignition sequence for the Beast's two multifuel engines. "Do you intend on telling the others about this development?"

Swash toyed with his com while watching Blade start up

his rover. "Not yet. Blade already knows we're headed for a garbage-can city. I'm sure I'll be getting an earful once we arrive. Best if he keeps his attention out for an attack by Inferno. As for Stitch and Whisper, I'd rather let them get a good sleep while they can."

23

Swash felt good to be on the move again. Blade had a point, rovers were meant to travel, not get stuck where they could be easily raided. He checked that his com was set to direct line of sight to the rig ahead then switched it to *All Users*. "Captain Blade, any word on our pursuers?"

"They're out there. I don't know where, but I can feel the danger."

Swash didn't press Blade for specifics. The back-of-the-neck, hair-raising intuition had alerted Swash to too many approaching disasters for him to discount the feeling in others. "I have another tactical piece of information. There's an old government installation buried behind the garbage-can city in Springs. It's deep inside the mountain. If the gen mods don't have what we need, we might have to consider breaking in."

Blade slowed the Desert Rat slightly. "Sounds like more than just a supply depot if it's inside the mountain."

"I don't have a good handle on what's inside the mountain, only that it existed at one time. There's also a strong possibility it could still be inhabited."

The rover ahead picked up speed again. "And you need me to figure out how to break in?"

"You are our militia expert. If we're correct, that place is going to be sealed tight. The gen mods might not even know about it."

"Speaking of our little furry friends, you do realize I might not be welcome in their compound, right?"

Swash wondered how long it would be before Blade brought up his battles with the 'monsters' as he called them. "You just make friends everywhere you go."

"So far at least you haven't tried to kill me."

"Just beat the snot out of you that one time. Okay. So, how bad is this situation going to be?" Swash considered flipping the com to private, but the others had a right to know what they were dealing with.

"I suppose we have the time. Before I get into it though, I've got a question. Any idea how long Springs has operated as a garbage-can city?"

Swash couldn't see why it would matter, but he made a quick check of his grandfather's log. "I can't be certain. Bullet said he'd been there as a teenager while it was a standard prison. That must have been around eighty or ninety years ago. He wasn't aware of it changing to a gen mod detention area, but based on how fast things fell apart back then, I'd guess around seventy years, give or take a decade. Why?"

"Seventy years." Swash could practically hear Blade running the numbers in his head. "Easily three generations."

Swash never could abide someone who didn't speak their mind. "So?" he prompted.

"And I'm guessing there's no way of knowing what type of gen mods got thrown in the garbage-can?"

"Out with it, Blade." Swash intentionally left off the captain designation.

"Fine. After my time with the religious zealots, I wasn't part of any damn military contingent, so I don't have any insider information. We were just raiders looking for easy scores. We didn't know reconstituted shit about garbage-can cities, only that the beings that lived there weren't human. My former experience had been mostly in how to exterminate them. With our raider arsenal, it seemed like easy pickings. On that point, we were completely wrong. We set up a remote-control truck to use as a battering ram. Instead of us swarming in for the surprise attack, however, they came out at us like we'd just kicked in a warrior hornet nest."

Swash's only surprise was that Blade hadn't expected a counterattack. "Did you really think they were such animals that they wouldn't defend their home?"

"Swash, I'm telling you. They weren't human. They weren't even like Roach, though some of them were. What did Whisper say Aural called them?"

"The spawn." Swash began to understand what worried Blade. Three generations of inbreeding between the original gen mods would likely result in biologically random offspring. "What did you see?"

"I'm not sure how to explain it. There was no uniform species. Some of them had similarities. The marauders I was with grouped them into categories. There were the flying monkeys, though they couldn't stay airborne for more than a hundred feet. They came in various sizes from much smaller than Roach all the way to ten-foot monsters. What I remember most were the teeth and claws. They came crashing out of the sky, intent on ripping flesh from bone. Then there were the ramrods. They were liked massively developed humans. I saw one plow straight into one of our trucks. Bent the radiator right around his lowered shoulder. He reminded me of something from sporting events from hundreds of years ago. But they were smart. They worked as a team. We never did fall one of them."

"Why didn't you tell me all of this sooner?" Swash wasn't sure what he'd have done with the information, but knowing about a threat was one of the main ways of staying alive.

"I haven't finished. There was also a group we called the shadows. I can't tell you what they look like. The images were removed from my mind, as they were for all of my compatriots. You see, I didn't tell you about these monsters because I believed, and still do, that I was hallucinating. Along with the horrid screeches and screams was a sound that was felt rather than heard. It gave us all pounding headaches. We only realized what had happened when we were safely out of their zone and we could compare notes. We all agreed there were other beings in the mix. The high-pitched noise they emanated created a psychosis in us. The overall effect isn't one I'd like to relive."

Swash drummed his thumbs on the steering wheel as he drove. "And you're worried the Springs will be filled with the same terrors?"

"After hearing about Whisper's encounter with Aural, I'm positive it will be."

SWASH LET BLADE take the lead through the mountains. The ancient network of roads had been heavily bombed during his grandfather's wars. The resulting blast cauldrons had filled with water from the last gasp of weather events before the climate upheaval. Ponds with surfaces of half an acre proved the perfect breeding ground for insects of all kinds. And the insects proved the perfect hosts for viruses. All Swash knew of the forest that had originally covered the area were the desiccated trunks and logs that provided homes to the bugs just waiting to be set loose. He followed Blade around a sinkhole of florescent green, the slippery and deadly algae being the next stage of the pit's evolution.

Swash activated his com to distract his attention from the scenery. "We're not far from the mountain pass. Whisper, once we get to the top I want to launch a long-range hawk drone to check the area. Strip it down of armaments. I don't want to give the garbage-can city any reason to attack. I just want a look at what we're dealing with."

"I'm just giving Whisper her final antipsychotic," Stitch said. "We'll have the drone ready."

Roach continued to operate the hummingbird drones

that provided information on the terrain ahead. "What's your plan?"

Swash removed his com, prompting Roach to do likewise. "If what Blade described is what we'll be dealing with, I don't think a frontal assault would do us much good. We need to negotiate with them."

Roach kicked his feet up onto the display, momentarily disrupting the three-dimensional image of a boulder coming up in their path. "A place like Springs might have the raw metal we'll need and hopefully the solar equipment, but military-grade batteries and plasma lances aren't the kind of thing a guard force is likely to leave behind for the inmates to use in a counterattack."

Swash had worried about the same issue. "We're going to need to get into that base. What's your take? Would the gen mods know they were sitting in front of the descendants of the very people who likely incarcerated them?"

"Not just imprisoned, boss. If that really is a refuge of last resort, whatever population escaped into that mountain was probably responsible for the whole damn genetic modification program, or at least had something to do with it. I can't imagine that would be the kind of people the gen mods of Springs would let peacefully coexist. So either they don't know about them, couldn't reach them, or the vault was raided long ago. Aural would lose his guano if he could lay his hands on that library."

Swash tried to stay focused. "Do you think that's why he sent Whisper the coordinates?"

"Seems likely. With his treasure trove of books, he might know about the hidden refuge. He clearly wanted something from Whisper. If his plan is for us to bust into that vault, maybe he'll provide us a positive reference with the inhabitants of Springs."

Swash wasn't prone to relying on hopeful thinking. "Even if he did, they'd likely just consider him some old hermit living in the mountains. I wouldn't put much trust in any endorsement he might or might not provide."

"Which gets us back to what you want to do."

Swash sighed as he watched Blade turn his truck toward an open space between the boulders. "Frontal assault is out. I strongly doubt they won't see us coming, so sneaking in won't work either. We'll need to approach their main gate and hope they don't preemptively attack."

Roach dropped his feet to the floor and leaned toward Swash. "Send me and Whisper. You could keep the Beast in some safe location a mile or so from the camp, and we can walk in."

Swash eyed Roach. "You'd have to do so without your bodysuit. That would mean giving away your secret to Cypress. She's the only one who doesn't already know you're a monkling."

He shrugged. "Time she found out."

24

Whisper looked out the front view screen of the Beast. The whole eastern half of the country seemed to spread out before her. "They know we're here." She'd been getting waves of headaches since leaving the caves. Slowly she was coming to realize they weren't random, but rather sonar induced.

"How do you know?" Roach had been his usual sweet self. Any moment that Stitch wasn't poking, prodding, or inoculating her, he had been at her side.

"I can hear their sonar."

Captain Swash eyed her with his usual intensity. "What are your friends saying?"

"It's not a language, and it's not the batlings. It's the bats themselves. I think they're being used as motion detectors, or maybe they're responding to me specifically. I don't know, but I can tell they're interested in what we're doing."

"Any idea if they're hostile?" Stitch asked.

"I don't think they are. It's more like curiosity, though I could be projecting that feeling."

The captain pointed at the drone controls. "Well, if they're checking us out, they shouldn't object to us doing the same. Launch the hawk drone and key in the Desert Rat. I want to get a look inside that camp. The more information Captain Blade has the better he'll be able to help if things don't work out in our favor."

After activating the rover-to-rover video link, Whisper engaged the joystick, lifted the drone from its cradle on the roof, and sent it on its way. "How do you want me to make the approach?"

"Stay low but find me a reasonable route for the Beast. Once you get close to the compound, circle up the mountain. I want to see if there are any indications of the military base under this pile of rocks."

Between the maps and the twin hummingbird drones holding position high overhead, Whisper had a pretty good idea of where the Beast might make its approach. She kept the oversized hawk drone at treetop level and soared it down the crest of the mountain. The first few miles proved uneventful. At ten miles the hawk exceeded the hummingbird's coverage. She angled the big drone lower down the incline for a better look at what remained of the interstate roadway. "Pretty beat-up landscape."

Captain Swash leaned in toward the display. "Give me a hundred-foot clearance of the trees and work your way back up to the ridge. I don't want to get stuck sneaking in below the camp."

Whisper nodded once and pulled back on the joystick.

"There." Roach pointed his finger into the projection. "I see something."

Whisper pulled the drone into a hover position above where Roach had indicated. "I don't see anything." She swung the camera into widening concentric circles.

Roach seemed locked onto a portion of the image. "Drop the drone between the remains of those two trees, halfway to the ground."

She knew better than to question whatever cute monkey-boy thought he'd seen. Carefully, to avoid getting the drone hung up on one of the desiccated limbs, she brought the large hawk down along the peeling gray bark.

"Stop." This time it was the captain who spoke. "Angle the camera ten degrees right and up just slightly."

"What are you two seeing?" Stitch asked to Whisper's relief. She couldn't figure it out either. The camera traced along the side of the tree and came to a stop.

"How in the world did you spot that, monkey-boy?" She zoomed the lens in on a bug that didn't look like anything she'd seen before. "I've never seen a death beetle with a fuzzy yellow body before."

Stitch leaned in. "That's because it isn't. I think that's a honey bee, but I'd heard they were extinct. Bees were killed off by chemicals during the country's so-called agricultural modernization. I suppose they could have survived up here, but there wouldn't be much for them to live off."

Roach continued to stare at the strange little bug. "At first I thought it was one of General Payne's glimmering robotic pollinators. That's why I pointed it out. If it's alive, something that alien in this landscape must have come from someplace else." He turned to Stitch. "What else do you know about these insects?"

She shrugged. "They were the primary pollinators of crops back when plants were still male and female. They lived in hives, so this little dude must not be alone."

The captain leaned back in the driver's chair and locked eyes with Whisper. "Finding the person in control of the satellites was only part of your mother's mandate. If I take what Stitch is saying to its logical conclusion, someone up here must be tending to these little creatures. Someone who needs them for their old-fashioned crops to survive. Do you think such information might get the Brigadier General off our backs?"

"It might." Whisper tried to sound more encouraging than she felt. "Though at best she'd consider it a consolation prize."

Roach pointed at the display. "Don't lose it."

Whisper had to act fast to track the insect that had taken flight. "Even if there is some magical farm out here, how would we find it?"

Captain Swash activated the bridge-to-bridge split-screen video link so the crews could see each other while still projecting the drone footage to the Desert Rat. "Captain Blade, do you think you could take over tracking our little friend out there?"

"This buggy didn't come with remote ops." The man didn't sound pleased. Whisper assumed he wasn't crazy about being demoted from warrior to science nerd.

Roach reached into the storage locker against the back wall of the bridge. "I've still got the handheld remote for the

Jump Spider. It'd only take a minute to modify it to run the hawk drone."

"Do it," the captain said. "It'll give Captain Blade something to do while he's keeping watch on us from the ridge." He turned back to the video display. "I can't exactly take you with us while we make contact with the garbage-can city."

Blade's scowl softened. "I suppose my reputation would precede me. From up top, I'll have a good vantage point in case things turn ugly. I concur with your recommendation, Captain Swash. I'll have Cypress map out the ridge while we're up there. Any idea what we should be looking for other than following that bug?"

Stitch bit her lip before answering. "I'd assume something like what Sky Payne showed us. Look for a valley or geological depression, something that would make for a natural protective petri dish for the agricultural experiment. I'll send over everything I have on bees."

"If we're going to do this, we'd better get moving," Blade said. "That hawk drone is already miles ahead of us. It'll be dark by the time you get to the village gates."

"Agreed," Captain Swash said. "Roach, get the remote over to Captain Blade, then you and Whisper get whatever rest you can. I need you both on top of your game when you approach Springs."

BLADE DID his best to avoid Cy's side-eye glare, but her huffs of annoyance and aggressive jamming of the remote-control joystick weren't as easy to ignore. "If you have something to say, say it."

"I didn't sign on to be relegated to chasing bugs like some silly little girl with a butterfly net."

"Like you'd know a butterfly if you saw one."

She looked over from the small handheld screen. "I've seen pictures."

Blade pointed at the remote. "Lose sight of that bug, and I'll institute corporal punishment on my rig."

She let out a single grunting laugh. "You haven't got the nerve." Even so, she did return to her duty. "I'm just saying, you're the weapons master around here, and I feel we've been sent on a mission designed to keep us out of the way."

Though he halfway agreed with her, admitting to it wouldn't do them much good. "If Swash is right, and if we can track that little yellow bugger back to his colony, we might finally get one step ahead in this tug-of-war for dominance with the Beast."

She furrowed her brow as she kept her gaze fixed on the remote screen. "How do you figure?"

"Think about it for a minute. If there is some weirdo out here growing crops, he's not making a lot of noise about it."

She kicked her feet onto the dashboard as she worked the joystick with more finesse. "Why would he? Attention would only make it harder to defend his plot of land."

"Exactly." Blade looked over at her to see if she'd catch his drift. "He'd only be selling to those who could help and protect him."

"You don't think he's selling to the gen mods?"

Blade let out a laugh of derision. "I'll bet you a month's

wages those mutants don't have enough to entice a lone raider out of the Great Pains."

She bit her lower lip as she looked up from the screen. "You think this farmer is supplying the hidden military installation?"

Blade went back to focusing on the uneven terrain. "I think that stupid little bug flying up ahead might prove to be our key to breaking into a vault filled with supplies, weapons, and ammunition. If we can get to the goodies before the Beast, we'll flip the power dynamic between our two rovers. We certainly can't face off against the mutants with what we've got. I think Swash is heading straight into a trap. I'd leave him to his own brand of destruction, but we still need the Beast's equipment for survival."

Cy slowly nodded. "So you think we can sneak into the back door of the military and just take what we want? They are the ones with the weapons, you know."

The plan was coming together in Blade's mind with such elegance that he could practically see the events unfold. "I think they've been down in those caves for generations. Even though it may have been a military base to start with, the refugees who escaped the apocalypse were political leaders and rich influencers. I imagine only a few of the original inhabitants were trained military personnel. There's probably a guard force of some sort, but they won't be battle hardened. It'll be like taking candy from a baby. Then we open the main hatch that leads into the back of the garbage-can city and stage our rescue. After that, Swash will have to submit to my authority."

"That's a lot of hope riding on delicate little wings."

"Possibly, but there's another thing I'd like to point out. A number of these hidden bunkers kept genetic material meant to be used to restart the environment should the climate ever stabilize. If Stitch's explanation is correct, then bees would be high on that list. I think it's more likely that our little friend up there came from a hive built in a lab than one that survived the apocalypse. I just hope they used the unadulterated DNA."

25

Stitch never wanted to be the voice of conscience for the crew, but nagging feelings had to be expressed. With Swash muscling the steering wheel of the Beast, aiming it ever higher up the mountain range, she worked the hummingbird drones along the ridge. "What happens when we get to the Springs, find it inhabited, and discover those in charge don't want to trade with us? We don't have that much to begin with, and from what I'm hearing we need a lot of hard-to-get items."

She watched Swash closely for any sign of deception. "Are you worried about me getting us into another fight?"

"Partly, but I'm more worried about who we're becoming. If we create a two-front attack with Blade, rush in with guns blazing, and steal what we want, how does that make us any different than the marauders we've encountered?"

Swash shook his head. "I brought you on as our medic, not some spiritual adviser."

She eased back in her seat and watched the terrain ahead. "You'd better get used to me being concerned about more than fixing your booboos. This growing relationship we've got going means I can't just turn and walk away if you take us in a direction I don't like."

"All I worry about is keeping us alive. I've never ransacked a place for personal gain, only as a last desperate attempt at survival. If you know a better way than what we've been doing, I'll be happy to listen."

"And Whisper?" Stitch felt like a lump of reconstituted and dehydrated shit was lodged in her stomach.

"What about Whisper?" Swash asked.

"She has the power to activate a satellite's arsenal. That's a lot to lay on a young woman's shoulders."

Swash lifted his foot slightly off the accelerator, slowing the Beast, as if the idea had caused him to lose focus. "I wasn't on board when it happened. From what I understand, Sky Payne turned loose of the reins to the satellite for that one strike. There's no reason to believe Whisper can just use the weapon whenever she likes."

"There's no reason to believe she can't," Stitch said. "That girl is wicked smart when it comes to finding her way around technology."

He nodded slowly as the Beast rolled over the uneven ground. "You're right about that. So you're saying I need to set a good example for the crew, or else I might end up creating a monster out of Whisper?"

"It doesn't take a genius to realize that she sees you as a father figure."

He glared over at her. "I'm the captain. I'm no one's *father*, figurative or otherwise."

She glared right back at him. "You know what I'm saying. What you say and do carries a lot of weight with Whisper."

He turned back to the view screen, but she could see the glare hadn't left his face. "What if I demanded she not utilize her special connection with the satellite?"

Stitch aimed the hummingbird drones higher into the sky as if there might be an answer on the horizon. "She'd listen, but your command would only last until one of us got into trouble that required a burst of lightning from the sky to resolve."

He sighed deeply. "And if we went foraging in camps, eventually we'd be right smack dab in the middle of just such a problem. You present a very forceful argument."

She wanted to reach over and touch his arm, but the two stations were too far apart. "I don't have an answer to my thought problem. I just needed to share it with you."

"Hopefully, Whisper's mother is as clever as her daughter. I can't see her just handing over a weapon that powerful without some form of failsafe against Whisper using it on a whim."

~

ROACH STEPPED onto the bridge just as Swash brought the Beast to a stop a couple of miles from the garbage-can city. "How do you want me to handle the negotiations, boss?"

Swash shut off the engines. "I've been working on that. We don't have much to offer. Hell, we're the ones coming in need of stuff. The first job in any encounter is to figure out what the other side needs and wants. Don't demand to see the person in charge. They're usually more concerned with remaining in power than satisfying the needs of the population. Talk to the people on the street. Find out what it's like to live there. We must have something to offer them."

"And if we don't?"

Swash turned his chair toward Roach. "Then we'll sneak in and take what we want, but that'll have to be our last resort. Your job is to make contact, inventory what they need, see what they have, and do a tactical analysis of the compound. Just make sure you two get out of there alive without kicking over the death-beetle nest. I don't need them swarming in on us."

"So basically we're going in as spies." Roach wasn't crazy about betraying his kind even if they weren't his family.

"I'm sending you in as emissaries. I'd like this to be beneficial to both sides."

Roach looked at the boss skeptically. "As you said, we don't have much on this rig to offer them. And we need quite a lot."

Swash frowned and nodded while looking down. "We may have one ace up our sleeve." He turned back to Roach. "From what I've seen, most garbage-can cities don't have much to begin with. I highly doubt they're going to have the kind of equipment we need to repair the Beast. If we're right about the military compound still being functional under the mountain, the gen mods might want to break into that treasure chest just as much as we do. Don't ask directly about what they know though. There's a good possibility that compound managed to remain a secret even to its closest neighbors."

"And Blade?" Roach was well aware of the warrior's distrust that bordered on downright hatred of gen mods.

Swash pointed to a spot on the ridge above the camp. "If I know our former weapons master, even now he'll be looking for a way into the military barracks. Between that, following the bee, and keeping an eye on us, he should be occupied enough not to stage a preemptive attack on Springs."

26

*B*lade held so tightly to the steering wheel of the Desert Rat that he feared his fingers might snap off from the tires' jarring feedback. The rocks and ruts that made up the terrain grabbed hold of the tires and tried to send the vehicle onto its side. He'd driven enough rovers to know that what he *felt* was as important, if not more so, than what he *saw* out the windshield. Again he closed his eyes and shook his head in an attempt to make sense of the terrain.

"What's wrong?" Cypress had an annoying way of asking exactly the wrong question at the wrong time. She needed to stay focused on following the bee, not be distracted by what she couldn't do anything about.

He nodded toward the windshield. "Tell me what you see."

She frowned and shrugged her shoulders. "Rocks and dirt. Why? What am I supposed to see?"

He locked his arms straight out toward the wheel, hoping the truck wouldn't be crushed by the cresting wave of landscape that was about to crash in from the side. "Nothing seems odd to you about the horizon?" To his relief and dismay, no avalanche of dirt and rock materialized to bury the truck.

Cypress leaned in toward the glass. "What the hell?"

"Tell me."

"It looks like the ridge is coming apart. Is it a volcano?" she asked.

Blade pressed the accelerator to the floor. "If it were, we'd be feeling it."

"Faulty view screen?"

He glared over at her. Even her face seemed to be losing its form. "The Desert Rat doesn't have a computerized view screen. It must be something in the air." When he turned back to the chaotic scene out front, instinct made him swing the steering wheel so violently that the truck swung up onto two wheels.

Cypress jerked up out of her seat and pulled on the air control levers. "I'm instituting air contamination protocols. Don't do anything stupid behind the wheel. It must be coming from outside."

He looked down at the scrolling map display. From the swinging cliffs that appeared to be closing in on the Desert Rat, it appeared the technology was as useless as his eyes. "I don't dare stop. If this is an attack, that's exactly what our pursuers would want."

Even in his peripheral vision he could tell she was closing one eye, staring intently, then doing the same with the other eye. "The path to the right looks clear. Straight ahead the ground is splitting wide open."

He did his eye squeeze again. Off to the right, a wave crest twice the height of the truck was about to drop human-sized boulders onto the roof of the cab. The ground in front swung violently from left to right. "I need drone support."

"I'm already using the remote ops to follow that little bee with the hawk drone, but I can try." She punched the eject button with the heel of her foot. From under the windshield, the small bundle of technology flew straight out, spun hard left, careened off a boulder, and fell to the ground.

"Why didn't you have that on object avoidance?" He knew irritation at the whole situation was getting the better of him, but if she was going to last long as his only crew member, Cypress was going to have to get used to his outbursts.

"I did. The damn thing must be suffering a technological version of what we're feeling. It must have sensed something in front of us."

"Straight ahead it is."

"No, any direction *but* straight ahead." Her shrill voice actually helped him think a little clearer.

"You, this stupid computer map, that drone, and my eyes all say the same thing. Straight ahead is disaster. That's how I know it's were we have to go."

Cypress leaned in toward the air vent, took a deep breath, then eased back into her seat. "You're right. Straight ahead is the only safe path. Someone sure is going to a lot of trouble to make us drive to our own destruction."

$\sim$

BLADE EASED the Desert Rat under the lip of a cliff—one tall enough to hide the rig from anyone poking around in the dead forest. The vista of the valley below only gave him a sliver view of the edge of the garbage-can city, but it did include the front gate.

"What are you doing? This isn't the time for admiring the view." Cypress continued stalking the little bee on her mobile drone display.

He ignored her outburst. "How did our little friend make out?"

"The drone or the bee? Near as I can tell they both must have flown high enough to escape whatever biological and technical manipulations we were encountering at ground level. The little critter zoomed into a large opening under that flat rock to the left. The entrance might barely be large enough for a human to squeeze through. Now do you mind telling me why we stopped like rabbits waiting for the coyote?"

He nodded toward the nearest tree trunk. "We're not alone. Those markings delineate a marauder boundary. Someone's claimed this area, and it's not the custodian of that little yellow dude you've been following."

"You think this is a trap?" Cypress finally sounded like she appreciated the danger and wasn't just being petulant.

"Why bother after all of the trouble they went through to destroy us?"

"I think someone was doing their best to keep us out of this area." He took the drone control from her hands and inspected the view screen. "There are blast marks down the hill from that cave." He swung the technobird away from the bee's lair and along a barely identifiable foot path. "Looks like someone was trying to lead a band of thugs away from the treasure chest."

"Can you tell how long ago?"

He checked the drone's display of options. "I probably should have paid more attention when Whisper explained this thing." He activated a sensor marked *Residual Energy*. The blast mark glowed red and orange with a scale illuminated at the bottom of the screen. "If I'm reading this right, it looks like the battle happened within the last twenty-four hours."

She snatched the remote control from his hands. "More like half an hour."

"How do you figure?"

She nodded toward a canyon below the ridge. Bursts of light indicated blasters. "Because our fugitive is still on the run."

Blade quickly ran through his options. Throwing in with the marauders could too easily alert Warlord Inferno or even the remains of Scorch's crew. But if they were going to save the fool on the run in an attempt at buying his favor, they were going to have to hustle. "Recall the drone."

"Recall the drone?" Her snarky attitude never fully left. "Are you crazy? It's the only eyes we have out there."

"It's also our best weapon once we re-arm it. Use the technobinoculars to keep an eye on the action while I load a blaster onto our bird." He unstrapped from the driver's seat.

"And what about the Beast?" she asked.

"Screw the Beast. Swash wanted us out of the action. That's why he sent us on this wild bee chase. If they get into trouble, I'm sure we'll hear about it one way or another." He took a breath to face his guilt. "Just the same, I want you to stay on the Desert Rat. If anything happens on the valley below, find a way to alert me. With you manning the drone, hopefully you can buy me enough time to work my way into the action. If we're going to gain this fracking fool's trust, one of us is going to need to be there for the rescue. No one trusts a drone."

"Then why not just drive in and save the day?"

He wondered if she'd been spending too much time with Swash's crew. "Because, my slave crewmember, any good marauder camp will have lookouts. This rig is worth a hell of a lot more than some fool biologist. We'd be driving straight into a trap. Now be a good little servant and do what I tell you!"

As BLADE SNUCK around the final boulder that separated him from the action, he wondered how saving people had become such a bad habit. The marauders' victim had wedged himself into a notch under a large rock outcropping. Though it was a defensible position, it was also one of last resort. With nine thugs hammering away with their blasters, he wouldn't last long. Fortunately for the fool, the hawk drone was peppering away at the thugs from behind.

Cypress's handling of the drone reminded him of how she flirted—buzz in, hit hard, then run off before having to face retaliation. At least she hadn't lost the drone. And so long as the goons were swatting away her advances, they wouldn't notice his attack. He twisted the barrel of his blaster to *Tight Beam*. The shots wouldn't be very impressive, but so long as he aimed at vital organs, they wouldn't have to be. A quarter-inch hole drilled straight through the heart was equally as deadly as a one-foot blast to the chest. It just didn't call as much attention to the one holding the weapon.

He laid flat on smooth rock and took careful aim at the goon closest to him and furthest from the action. One shot to the temple and the guy slumped to the ground without uttering a sound. The drone dropped in altitude and hovered farther to the left of the action. Any shot Cypress took and missed would carve into the strewn boulders, and not Blade. *Thanks for that.* He mentally stored the compliment for when it might be needed to get her off his ass.

She fired wildly as if power consumption wasn't an issue. The guy in the rocks was much more deliberate with his shots, but unfortunately not any better of an aim. As Blade took out the second of his targets, he estimated they'd fired seven discharges. And for all of the spent energy, they'd landed one goon between them. At that rate, both of their weapons would be drained of energy before they'd even landed half of the attack force. Not that how many they killed mattered so long as their concerted attack kept Blade's presence unknown to the marauders, but it did mean he didn't have time to spare.

Blade's third shot hit his target, but because of a last-moment spin by the fracker, he only drilled a clean hole through the idiot's shoulder and missed the heart.

The goon lifted his functional arm and let loose a blast that singed Blade's scalp. "We're in a crossfire," he yelled after the shot.

The remaining six marauders formed a triangle, two to a side to cover each other, and dropped to the ground. Blade twisted his blaster to *Full Coverage*. His next shot blinded and scorched the two facing him. From the wildly inaccurate return fire, he knew he'd seriously injured both of them but hadn't killed either one. He jumped to his feet and took them out from above with a prolonged spray of plasma.

Cypress on the drone took out a combatant as well, but at the expense of the drone. The large flying gun platform tumbled to the ground a hundred yards from the action. From the lack of fire from under the cliff, Blade assumed his objective had run out of firepower too. *Well, at least I'm down to three. Easy odds.* He walked straight at the remaining goons as they tried to figure out where to attack next. The delay cost them another member of their tribe.

A rogue shot to the left arm and side of his chest sent Blade spinning to the ground. He landed with his weapon still aimed at the last two marauders. Planning, tactics, and careful aim only took him so far. Firing all he had in a fit of anger often worked just as well or even better. When his eyes cleared, he saw the final two idiots as nothing more than smoking embers. A quick look to the hiding place in the rocks made it clear the guy they'd rescued had flown the coop. *Frack.*

27

Blade bristled at having Cypress tend to his wounds. "I'll be fine if you'll just stop poking me!"

"You can be such a baby at times. Put your arm up and let me get this technogauze around your chest."

Her bedside manner left him wanting to spank her, or fuck her, he really couldn't decide which. But sitting in the crew quarters of the Desert Rat in nothing but his shorts made him feel like a little boy who'd fallen while playing commando. "Maybe if you hadn't lost the drone we'd know which way our prey had headed."

"Just trying to save your ornery hide. If those jacked-up marauders hadn't been shooting their loads at me, they might have had enough juice to burn half your leathery hide to a crisp. So what's your next brilliant plan, *Captain*?"

He really wasn't in the mood for her attitude. "Well,

slave, without the drone and no guide, I guess we'll have to explore the cave that little bee disappeared into."

She stood up straight and put her hands on the hips of her agroleathers. "I think that'll do. Just don't go doing something stupid for the next six hours. According to the package that's how long it will take to heal your burns." She looked out the front windshield. "Don't you think we should check in on the Beast? I'd like to get confirmation from Stitch that you're going to be okay."

"I do not think we should check in with the Beast. In fact, that's probably the last thing we should do. Those marauders will have friends around here somewhere. Broadcasting a signal would only lead them straight to us. I'm certain Swash has things under control."

"Really? Like you're certain you're going to be just fine?" she asked.

He got up and stretched his shoulder. The gauze pulled at his damaged skin. From the tightness in his muscles they felt like they'd fried to a medium rare. Since his arm responded, he assumed they were still attached to the bones. The fracking med-nanites made the whole side of his body tingle. "Exactly. Now pack a kit. I want to get up to that cave before dark, and we can't risk driving the Desert Rat."

THE CLIMB HAD PROVEN MORE painful than Blade had anticipated, not that he let any of his groans, missteps, or soaked bandages become obvious to Cypress.

"It looks tight, but I think I can squeeze in. Why don't

you wait here?" She had a look of concern that irritated him even more than the technogauze.

He pushed her out of the way. "And let you have all the fun? Besides, if that little bee's stinger is the worst we have to fear in there, I'll let you drive the Desert Rat for the next month."

She peeked around him into the darkness. "And if I lose?"

"You have to be nice to me."

She crossed her arms and looked into his eyes. "No bet. But I will let you go first if for no other reason than to see you try to hide the pain."

He couldn't fault her play. Truth was his body hurt like hell. *Those damn little nanites must be past their expiration date.* He prodded at his shoulder before getting on his belly. The gap was barely large enough for him to squeeze into, but he managed.

"I sure hope you don't land in a bee hive. From Stitch's information, they like to live in a great big commune. The queen runs the show, and all the little males die after mating with her. Sounds like my kind of arrangement. No wonder men killed them all off."

He turned his head in the tight space to glare at her. "Bees wouldn't set up camp in this desolation. There has to be some kind of oasis in this cave. Now unless you have something useful to contribute, shut up so I can focus."

"I'm just saying, being queen of a colony doesn't sound like a bad gig to me."

He scuttled further along into the cave as much from curiosity as to what lay ahead as annoyance with her. The tunnel, though not tall, proved to be wide enough for easy passage. He did his best to not see the passage as some type of cavernous mouth out to swallow him whole. "So far so good. You shouldn't have too much trouble." As the scraping sounds of agroleathers against stone announced her entrance, he pulled his body around a curve in the passage. Instead of the cave growing darker, however, lights illuminated a huge cavern. "I think we found what we were looking for."

BLADE STOOD at the lip of the concrete rim that stretched around the old sports complex. Metal ribs sored over the city-sized depression supporting the computer-controlled sky panels. "This must have been one of the last great arenas. I'd heard they were built in natural geological formations. A couple of good blasts must have collapsed the roof and flattened the original entrances."

Cypress dumped the backpack at their feet. "Looks like it's gone to shit."

He wondered if she'd ever played sports, but he didn't see the point in getting into a long conversation about the silliness of competing for the enjoyment of it. "This is definitely more plant life than I've ever run across. Seems unlikely to be here without someone taking advantage of the situation."

She fished in the pack for a hummingbird drone and the helmet remote control. "You want a better look?"

The idea had its merits. With one quick fly around, he

could map out the access points and likely fire up whatever security system was in place to keep the riffraff out. "Where'd you get that?"

"Stole it from the Beast. They had a whole crate of them. I doubt they'll even notice it's missing."

He shook his head. "Knowing Swash, he probably has an itemized inventory of everything on board that rover." He looked over the huge bowl of vegetation. "Better keep the drone in the pack. I wouldn't want to alert anyone to our presence."

"So what's your plan, Captain?"

He pulled out his technobinoculars and scoped out the old bench seats, stairs, and rotting structures. Though everything was covered in vines, at least the observation area was still terraced. The playing grounds, however, were so densely packed with plant life that it was impossible to see what creatures might be lurking in the jungle. "I'm going down there. Keep your earbud in. If you see anything, don't keep it to yourself."

She checked the communication device. "Be careful, okay?"

The show of concern made him look away from the technobinoculars. "We'll stay in contact. I'll keep you informed of everything I see."

She glared at him, but her look seemed to be less annoyance than worry. "I don't like this plan of yours. You could be walking right into a marauder's camp or worse."

Next to his foot a bee buzzed out of a flower and zoomed down toward the valley floor. "Marauders don't have access to original biological material. There's a scientist down there somewhere. I'm sure of it. But even he would need access to a seed vault. The only stash of original biological material would be in the military stronghold. Our little buddy flying around down there is our best indication that we're onto something."

"I'm giving you three hours. After that I'm sending the drone in after you. And if you don't talk to me for over an hour, you'd better be dead if you know what's good for you."

WITH EACH STEP, Blade's boot sunk through the terraced root and soil labyrinth clear down to the crumbling concrete step. Vines covered the rusted metal railing, threatening to entangle his hands as the roots did the same with his feet. The descent to the stadium floor-turned-jungle would be slow going. "Since a surprise attack appears out of the question, I'm going to start chopping my way through this foliage."

"Any indication of lifeforms more advanced than insects?" Cypress asked over the com.

He lifted his technobinoculars from his chest and dialed the computer enhancements to detect heat and movement. "I can't make out anything through all of these leaves. If this place is being tended by someone, they're doing a piss-poor job of it."

"A mercenary with a blaster isn't my only concern. If this place is some holdover from nature, who knows what animals might lurk in the shadows." Her concern sounded genuine.

Blade still couldn't see how that was possible, but he scanned higher up the spindly trees just the same. "I'm gonna work my way down to the floor. If I see anything, I'll let you know; otherwise I'll contact you in half an hour. It'll likely take me that long to get off these goddamn steps." He dialed down the volume on the com so he could focus on not losing his footing and tumbling down the remaining five stories of elevated seating. "While I'm doing that, you work your way around the lip. There has to be another entrance somewhere."

"I'll try, but from the collapsed beams and torn-up deck, I'd guess the roof pancaked all the way down to the top floor."

"Do what you can, and don't get caught." Cubicles containing discarded view screens originally intended for watching the sporting action lay along each terrace that stretched out on either side of his descent. The original chairs served as potting containers for the overflowing vegetation. Water dripped from the bottom of the seats into the mat of ferns and mosses that seemed to cover every inch of concrete. The lower he got from the rim the more humid the air became. He slowed his pace to combat the feeling of drowning. His skin slipped along the inner lining of his combat agroleathers.

"If I do run across someone, I'm going to have a tough time defending myself." He slashed at a tenacious vine that had wound around his ankle.

"Did you check your blaster?" Even with the earbud turned down, Cypress's voice rattled in his ear.

"I was talking to myself, but you make a good point. This

humidity isn't something me or my equipment are used to." He reached for his weapon.

"I can't let you do that." The voice came from above and behind his left shoulder.

He fought the urge to draw the blaster and swing around toward his adversary. Instead he lifted his hand from the butt of the blaster. "I'm not looking for trouble."

"That's what everyone says when they're at the disadvantage. Pull your gun and set it on the seat to your right." The lack of a threat should he not comply could either mean the man was unarmed or so sure of his advantage that he didn't feel the need to drive the point home.

Blade slowly withdrew the blaster and carefully nestled it into the plant stems. "This is some place you've got." He made the comment loud enough for Cypress to hear in the com.

The com clicked once in response. To her credit, she kept her yap shut. It wasn't like she could do anything about the situation. He just needed to make sure she was listening.

"Do you mind if I turn around?" Blade asked.

"Slowly, and keep your hands out where I can see them."

The vines tugged at Blade's feet as he shuffled against the wet concrete, reminding him of his precarious situation. As he expected, the first thing he noticed was the man's weapon. The rifle blaster's long barrel gleamed in the dim light. "My name's Blade. I've got a friend on the rim. We came from our rover, the Desert Rat, which is parked a few miles down the mountain." He didn't see any point in hiding his situation. Judging from the condition and caliber of the weapon, the man likely had other military equipment at his disposal. No mercenary simply had one badass blaster. Foremost in that bag of tricks would be reconnaissance gear. With any luck, the man might interpret Blade's openness as a desire for peace.

"I am Capote." By not offering any more information than strictly needed, it was up to Blade to either speculate on what other force might be hiding in the bushes or venture to ask the question outright.

Blade doubted he'd get an honest answer, not that it mattered. He wasn't in a position for battle. "Quite the greenhouse you've got here." He couldn't be sure if this was the dude he'd try to rescue or part of the contingent that was out to kill him.

"Not many stumble into it uninvited."

Blade nodded at a bee pollinating a bright purple flower of a vine growing around the partition next to Capote. "Your little friend there showed me the way." He wanted to drill the guy on how he snuck up behind Blade so easily, but these monster stadiums had all kinds of hidden passages, lifts, and secret access points—none of which Capote was likely to divulge. And where there was one obvious mercenary, there was likely a hole platoon in hiding.

Capote shook his long black hair behind his back then pulled a blade of grass out from the floor and stuck it between his teeth. "You must want something to have climbed down here."

If Blade could elicit enough information out of him, maybe they could get Whisper's pain-in-the-ass mother off their backs—or at least fabricate a convincing cover story.

"We have a friend whose farm is failing. From the existence of the bee, I'd hoped this jungle was actually some kind of agricultural experiment. I can see I was mistaken."

Capote's all-black eyes never left Blade's. "You're the guy who blasted those marauding idiots who were out to kill me." It wasn't a question. It also wasn't a thank you.

"You're welcome." Blade decided to tug on the thin string of the guy's good will.

"I suppose I owe you something." Capote pulled the stem from his mouth. "Describe the farm."

"Well, it doesn't look anything like your operation."

The man chuckled as he continued to cradle the plasma rifle. "Let me guess. One large field of a uniform crop with all of the plants neatly spaced and being tended by small robotic pollinators?"

"Pretty much," Blade said.

"And they've stopped germinating?"

"Exactly."

Capote reached down and pulled two flowers off neighboring plants. They looked nearly identical. "Your friend's first problem is a lack of bio-diversity. Before the apocalypse, farmers could get away with large single-crop fields. There were enough invasive weeds, treed wind breaks, and wild fields to provide the raw biological material to keep the crops on their toes. But if all a plant has for pollination is its own kind, the natural response is dormancy or sterilization."

Blade had done enough farming to know when a fellow farmer was about to go on a long-winded rant. "The back-to-nature philosophy hasn't worked so well. Plants breed with their own kind. That's just basic science."

The man set the back of his hand against the purple flower. A bee crawled onto him. "Take my little friend here. He travels all around my Eden sucking nectar from all types of flowers. And at each stop he picks up a few grains of pollen." He turned his wrist to show the powdery yellow balls on the insect's legs. He then held up a neighboring flower for the bug to climb into. "Right now this flower is being bombarded with dozens of different species of pollen. Somehow the plant figures out which one will germinate its seeds. But in doing so, the plant is also given a field guide of what lives around it—plants that will be beneficial, plants that will be harmful, even what diseases and pests are in the area." He twirled the flower causing the bee to fly away. "This flower just received an education better than the best human university." He picked up the matching flower and held them together. "But simply use plant A to pollinate plant B of the same species, and you get a dangerously unprotected and weak crop. You might as well just clone the plant."

A shiver went down Blade's back. "And we both know how well that worked out."

Capote nodded. "A disease that would normally only kill a small percentage of a field's plants suddenly becomes lethal to the entire crop. So you see the need for bio-diversity. At their basic biology, plants understand the threat as well. Shutting down the reproductive cycle is their form of a failsafe."

Blade put his foot on the concrete ledge the man was

sitting on and leaned in. "I don't see this Garden of Eden coming about naturally, and you couldn't have saved all of these plants all on your own. Who's behind this project?"

"You're not really in a position to make demands." From Capote's relaxed position, Blade assumed he was being watched from multiple locations. "You saved me, and I appreciate the effort. But that doesn't mean I'm handing you the keys to the kingdom."

"I'm just curious. The more I understand of this place the better I can help the failed farm. How do you know so much about ancient agriculture?"

Capote nodded toward the rim of the structure. "My people were the Ute Indians. We've lived off this land for centuries. There are only scatterings of us left." He waved his hand around the valley. "This started as an agroexperiment by a military science expedition. They hoped to restart the food chain. They failed. Their attempts at farming proved far too dependent on agrochemicals. At the time, the last of my family scratched out a living among the caves of the ancients. The military recruited farmers like my father to help with their project in exchange for all the food we would ever need. All they required was privacy and a portion of the crop."

Blade tried to control his excitement. "What became of the military contingent?" Though he didn't expect a straightforward answer, he hoped to get some indication of the base under the mountain.

"We have an understanding." The vague answer only confirmed what Blade had already figured out from

THE ROAD TO SURVIVAL

Capote's plasma rifle. The military thugs were still around somewhere.

"So you started learning about plants from your people then progressed to being a farmer and finally developed some knowledge working with the military's agriculturalists?"

"My father worked with the original agriculturalists." Capote looked out over the jungle. "Mostly I learned from tending these plants."

"And one day you'll extend this garden outside of this dome?"

Capote shook his head. "These are original generation plants. They'd never handle the intense solar radiation and chemical-laced rains. There are water lines that run along the trusses, fed by an aquafer far underground. By being under this sky dome, the amount of light and water they receive is regulated by computers. The rock-covered dome also protects the plants from chemical precipitation and hides the jungle from any wandering satellite."

Blade filed the additional confirmations in his memory. Original plant DNA had to come from a seed bank, and the same hidden spring that watered Capote's garden was likely what provided water to the inhabitants of the bunker. If there was one. He needed to gain access to what lay beyond the plant stadium if they had any hope of rebuilding the two rovers. His best shot was to gain Capote's trust. "Before I became a mercenary and rover, I was a farmer myself, though nowhere near as accomplished as you are. In my experience, there were never enough hands to tend to the crops. Would an exchange of labor for education be too presumptuous?"

Capote finally took the rifle from his lap and leaned it against the green-stained plastic partition. "I've just started the harvest. I suppose I could use some help. The offer would have to include your friend. I can't afford to have a stranger lurking around outside of the dome. And know that you'll always be watched. The sky dome is filled with eyes and ears. You'll get your weapons back when you leave the dome. That's our means of security. Without a blaster, you'd be easy prey outside of this structure."

"How do you go about transferring your crop to your landlords?"

Capote looked to the dome as if expecting fire from above for any betrayal. "I never see them. You'll leave your baskets of produce at the bottom of the stairs. Be back at your rover before dusk. At night, the bounty will be collected." He turned back to Blade with obvious fear in his eyes. "You don't want to be in the fields after it gets dark. Ghosts roam the grounds."

28

The longer the co-captain status went on, the less Swash liked the idea. Blade made a semi-reliable weapons master, but having the mercenary free to do as he pleased made planning a near impossibility. "Ping him again."

Stitch messed with the drone control. "I've already tried to raise him five times. I'm telling you I don't see any movement at all. The Desert Rat is just sitting there deserted."

"If that fracker went on some wild goose chase and left us unprotected, I'm going to kick that leathery hide—"

"Please stop." Stitch raised the hummingbird drone another hundred feet and made a slow rotation. "I'm detecting bodies a half mile from the rig."

Somehow Swash just knew anywhere Blade stayed for long would be marked with dead bodies. "Check it out. I just hope they aren't Blade and Cypress."

The image on the display screen whooshed by so fast it made Swash rub his eyes. "Doesn't look like it," Stitch said. "I count nine dead. From their mismatched combat agroleathers and worn weapons, they appear to be marauders."

Swash leaned closer to the display. "Look at their position and the blackened earth. They were caught in a crossfire, and not just from two positions. Looks like Blade and Cypress picked up a friend."

"Or a collaborator we didn't know about. Jeez. Listen to me. I'm starting to sound like you."

He nodded. "It never hurts to consider all perspectives. He was with a band of marauders for a lot longer than he was with us. It would make sense that he'd find his old crew eventually."

"Yeah, but it's the marauders who are dead."

He knew she was right. The scene didn't make sense. "Well, Blade and Cypress don't appear to be dead. At least not from this fire fight. But they're also not back at the rig. And there's some unknown addition to the duo."

She turned toward him. "You don't think they actually found the bee's nirvana, do you?"

He hadn't meant to send Blade on a fools errand, but he wasn't sorry to have him out of sight from the gen mod city either. "And this mysterious other combatant is part of the hidden farm? Seems farfetched, but we've seen stranger things lately. Whatever their situation is up there, we'd better plan on being on our own."

ROACH KEPT hold of Whisper's hand as they approached the old prison gate. He didn't know what to expect. From his experience growing up in a similar ghetto, the residents distrusted anyone they didn't know, even if that person was a fellow gen mod. "Let me do the talking. At least I look like a gen mod. They might not be as receptive to you."

"Do you think they'll be hostile?"

He pounded on the rusty metal plate that served as the entrance. "Only one way to find out."

Half a dozen bats flew in from the trees, nearly grazed Roach's head, and shot over the fence. "What do you want?" a voice boomed from the guard tower.

Roach backed up a few paces so he could look up into the lookout perch. "We're rovers in need of supplies."

"You've come to the wrong enclave. Best you turn around and look elsewhere."

Roach had expected the initial brush-off. "We have a proposition for whoever's in charge."

"We do?" Whisper's voice was so quiet it sounded like a breath of wind.

He squeezed her hand once to get her to keep quiet. "What could it hurt to talk?" he yelled to the sentry. "We're just two travelers."

"And what about the earth rover you left a mile down the road?"

Roach wondered if they didn't know about Blade, Cypress, and the Desert Rat or were just playing it cagy. "My captain and medical officer are on board that rig. They aren't gen mods. My friend and I are. We hoped that might help gain us entry. We just want to talk. If we can't help each other, then we'll be on our way."

There was a brief pause. Then the sounds of chains and gears preceded the heavy doors opening just enough for a skinny person to pass through. "Send in your friend first. If she checks out, we'll look you over as well."

Whisper let go of Roach's hand and stood a little straighter. He recognized her stance of determination. "I'm coming in," she said before he could stop her. He'd have rather been the first to go in just in case something didn't feel right.

No sooner had she slid between the metal doors than she was whisked to the side and out of sight. It took all he had to resist rushing in after her. "What are you doing to her?" The door closed to the mere sliver of a gap.

Light reflected off the barrel of the blaster the sentry had trained on Roach. "A simple DNA test to determine whether she's truly a gen mod. If she is, we have a couple of questions and the ability to determine whether she's telling the truth. If she isn't one of us, she'll be returned to you."

Roach didn't like waiting, especially when Whisper was involved. "At least let me be with her."

"This won't take long."

It seemed to take forever. Roach shuffled his feet in the ash and dust, wondering if the gen mods had anything worth risking Whisper's life over. He strongly doubted it. Finally, the door reopened. "Your turn."

He resisted the urge to run into the gap. As he slipped between the inch-thick steel doors, a knife was pressed to his throat and a needle plunged into his neck. "What's your name and business?" The needle was pulled out.

He hoped the needle was simply to draw blood for the completely unnecessary DNA test. "My name is Roach. We're here to negotiate for supplies." As he rubbed the puncture, Whisper slipped her hand around his upper arm and hugged him close.

"What are you looking for?" The guard kept to the shadows, preventing Roach from getting a good look at his interrogator.

"More than you have."

From the high-pitched chuckle that answered, Roach figured he was dealing with a batling. "And what are you offering in exchange?"

"Less than you need."

"Sounds like a typical rover." The being stepped out into the light.

Roach estimated the creature as being seven feet tall but no more than two-hundred pounds. Short bristly brown-and-gold hair covered every inch of exposed flesh. His sharply drawn black eyes stared out of aquiline facial features like burned out blasters. As Roach continued his inspection, the creature extended boney wings from behind his back. The flesh stretched thin and translucent, holding the joints connected. From the many tears in the membrane, Roach doubted the being could fly. "Who are you?" Roach's question could have just as easily been, *what are you?*

"They call me Bones. Since you and your friend check out as gen mods, you're both welcome in Sanctuary."

Roach figured pressing the guy on his heritage would be considered rude, so he moved on to his next set of questions. "What can you tell me about this place?"

Bones extended a wing down the dusty street like it was a giant finger. The joints made the popping sounds of arthritis. "We can talk as I show you around."

"You're a spawn, aren't you?" Whisper asked.

Bones walked with a slight stoop while holding the edges of his wings. Roach had once seen an educator in the Basin where he grew up use a similar stride while thinking. "My mother was a monkling, though of a larger breed than Roach. She was an imposing being. Many feared her. My father was closer to your evolution. He had some batling characteristics, but mostly he appeared human."

"Are they still alive?" Whisper's questions made Roach cringe. Where he'd grown up it was considered inappropriate to press a person on their heritage.

"No, dear. They died many years ago. They were among the second generation of gen mods to occupy Sanctuary. The original unfortunates were incarcerated here simply for being non-human."

"How old is this place?" Roach asked.

Bones looked toward the sky. "Must be over a hundred years now that gen mods have held control of Sanctuary. We welcome all gen mods, though we have little to offer beyond safety. In this area, out in the open, our kind are still hunted down like an invasive species."

"Do you run Sanctuary?" Whisper asked.

"No one *runs* Sanctuary. We live in peace with each other. Jobs that need doing either get done, or they don't

THE ROAD TO SURVIVAL

and we all suffer. After a hundred years, we've learned it's better to attend to a situation before it becomes a problem. We maintain a council for disputes, but it doesn't need to meet often. Someone always watches the main gate in case visitors like yourselves stumble into our midst. That person usually takes it on themselves to introduce the strangers to our way of life. Then they either stay or they leave."

The system seemed far too utopian for Roach to accept, but he didn't see any purpose in digging into the specifics. "What do you know of Sanctuary before the gen mods took over?"

"It was a place of horrors. We've erased everything of that time."

Including the name, Roach thought. It was going to be hard to find the entrance to the military base if the gen mods had intentionally deleted all they could of that past. The road that ran inside of the crushed-car wall diminished to a walking path. Every few hundred feet they passed another hovel slapped together from parts of buildings. Doors were nailed together to create walls. Sheets of corrugated metal seemed to be the roofing of choice. The size and shape of the dwelling looked to be designed to accommodate the individual spawn's dimensions and needs. Roach didn't see many inhabitants. "Where is everyone?"

Bones scrunched up his face. "Look around you. Would you want to bring a child into this misery? We live off what we can find in the old city, and that dwindling stash is less palatable each year. Every new birth results in another unforeseeable mutation. Some of us aren't even capable of reproduction. Child bearing is seen as an act of supreme arrogance and stupidity."

Stitch had warned Roach and Whisper about the dangers should their relationship result in an offspring. The medical officer had done all she could to prevent that from happening. Now Roach could see why. They climbed a winding trail to the top of a small hill that overlooked the old city of Springs. "If people are free to do as they want, why build these hovels when there's a whole city of homes to occupy?"

"Radiation, diseases, chemical disinfectants that proved a little too effective—the list of what makes the valley uninhabitable for my kind is quite long."

And that's probably where we need to start looking for the military access point, Roach thought. "So no one goes down there?" The smell of burned rubber that wafted up from the valley stung Roach's eyes.

"Just to hunt for supplies and building materials. But if you're thinking of exploring the area, you should be aware of the mongrels."

"Mongrels?" Whisper asked in a trembling voice.

"Not all unions of gen mods result in intelligent beings. Even among us monsters there are worse monsters. The creatures that prowl the streets down there are the main reason spawn like me refuse to mate."

"I'm beginning to see why not all of your visitors decide to stay," Whisper said.

Roach surveyed the area below. Nearly every car and truck on the streets had been reduced to blackened frames. Still, given the time he felt certain he could find what he needed to build another jump spider, providing of course he could survive the adventure. "I'm looking for car parts. What would Sanctuary's take be on me raiding the old city for what I need?"

Bones hunched his skeletal wings. "There's no ownership down in the valley, but getting the parts away from the mongrels would be a challenge. The longest any of us have remained in the old city is a day. No one's braved the area after dark."

"Why don't they come up here?" Whisper asked. "You are their parents."

"We don't have anything they want, and their emotional attachment is nearly reptilian. No matter how much we cared for them, eventually every mongrel born to my people ended up running away to join the packs below. I suppose they find a sense of belonging down there that they couldn't achieve with us. And just because we stopped breeding to avoid the inevitable, that logical restriction doesn't work for the mongrels. In another generation, they'll be the dominant force here."

Roach figured he'd seen all that he needed to. "We have information about a hidden military storehouse that might prove useful to both of us. We'd need your help to get in though."

Bones turned away from the smoldering remains of the old city. "Where?"

"We don't have a specific location, but my bet would be down in that valley. If we're going to find it and break in, you'll need to let my human friends into Sanctuary."

Bones frowned then shook his head in apparent

resignation. "Get your friends. I'll convene the council. It'll take much of the day tomorrow to round everyone up and decide if we want to meet your originals. I can't guarantee a meeting with my people, but be at the gate by late afternoon."

29

Cypress kicked the woven basket filled with vegetables. "So now I'm a fracking farmer's wife? Are you kidding me?"

Blade knew putting her to work tending plants was going to be a tough sell. He just didn't realize it was one he'd have to make continuously during this stage of the plan. "The faster you fill that basket the sooner we can haul our crop to the pickup point." He nodded toward the collapsed broadcast booth then snuck under the rotting beam. "Hand me your earbud."

She followed him in and pulled it out from behind her dirt- and sweat-coated blond hair. "What are you going to do with it?"

"I'm going to stick it up this peach's ass. With the drone remote, you should be able to identify its location. It's not like we can talk over the com link in this dome anyway without tipping off our adversary. Might as well put it to some use. I'll hang onto mine just in case we need it later."

"That's not a half-bad idea. Too bad we won't have a way of seeing where it goes."

He shoved the piece of plastic into the juicy pulp then buried the fruit deep in the basket of produce. "I'm not even sure this will work. There's a strong probability we'll lose the signal as soon as it's taken into the bunker. At least it might reveal the way to the access point."

She shook the basket of real food. "We're about half full. Any ideas on what else is edible in this section of the dome?"

Blade stepped out of the shelter and used the technobinoculars to identify the tubers, stalks, leaves, and hanging fruits. "According to Capote we should focus on anything hanging from vines or trees first. Looks like if we head deeper into the dome we might run across some older growth vegetation."

She grabbed a cucumber out of the basket and took a bite. "I could get used to this dirt food. At least he let us eat what we find. Though a place to rest would have been nice."

Blade was used to sleeping when and where he found the state of unconsciousness unavoidable. Day or night didn't matter much when death was a constant threat. "I don't plan on being here long enough for that to matter." He slung the basket over his shoulders. Even through his agroleathers, the wicker scratched at his legs. "There are plenty of old structures around to take cover from the waterings if you need a break. I want to get to the produce pickup site before late afternoon."

Cypress turned a full 360 degrees looking around the dome. "Have you seen anyone else?"

"Just Capote, but I haven't seen him since we started picking. We're supposed to meet up with him at dusk where we first met to collect our weapons. He seemed pretty freaked about being here after dark. I can feel others. We're not alone." The feeling wasn't something he could defend, however. It was the same sneaky sensation he got when he was walking into an ambush.

She nodded. "This place gives me the creeps."

Blade kept his head down, focusing on the mat of leaves, roots, and vines and kept his voice low. "From what I've seen, security around here is pretty lax. I suppose they feel being without a weapon puts us at their mercy. A hundred years of hiding has a way of dulling the protective reflex. On our way out, we'll stash the drone high enough in the dome to read the stadium floor. If our prey picks up our sneaky peach, we should have the entrance location soon enough. Once we have it mapped, you hightail it back to the Desert Rat. Swash is probably sweating bullets at not having cover. You'll have to soothe his frayed nerves. I'll set my ear com somewhere inconspicuous then work my way to the access point. Once you get back to the Desert Rat, send a drone outside the dome but in line with the com to relay the signal. When I find our wayward peach, I'll use that com to reach you. I just hope Roach and Whisper have success recruiting the gen mod community."

"What do you want me to tell Captain Swash?"

"To be ready."

"Do you really think he's going to listen?" she asked. "As you said, we did kind of leave him fully exposed."

Blade leaned over far enough for a dozen fruits and vegetables to tumble out of the basket on his back. "Send him a fruit basket."

CYPRESS LEFT the dome feeling a combination of frustration and admiration for Blade. She hadn't dared ask how exactly she was supposed to send a bag of food down to the Beast. *If this relationship is going to work, I can't constantly rely on my sexual prowess to tame him.*

Though she was confident she could manipulate her captain while riding in the Desert Rat, the same wasn't true if she wasn't commanding his full manly attention. She tried dusting the dirt off her pants, but the black stuff seemed to penetrate every fiber and pore. Not that her condition would have mattered. While in warrior mode the man was a rock, and not rock-hard in frustration like she liked him.

She pulled the last small drone from her pack and lined it up between the Desert Rat and the interior of the dome. Before lodging it in the crook of a tree limb, she turned the small orb in her hand. "You'd be too small to carry anything, but your big sister might." She limbed the lower branch and snugged the drone in place. Before climbing down, she scanned the area in search of the previous battle. She spotted a glint of light off the downed hawk drone.

In less than half an hour she'd secured the damaged bird,

returned to the Desert Rat, and secured a sling for carrying the food. What she couldn't do was fix the fracked-up electronics. She needed Roach. He'd help her without question, but she'd have to settle for Captain Swash. Instead of turning the communications dish toward the garbage-can city, she aimed it toward the Beast. "Desert Rat to Beast."

She heard the customary two clicks indicating she was heard but wouldn't be vocally acknowledged in case there were others listing in. She took the hint.

"I have a package and a message. I'm clear on this end."

The stern man's grumble preceded his words. "Status report."

She gritted her teeth. Obviously he knew about their lack of protection. "You're in the clear. No marauders are detected."

She could practically hear his thoughts regarding what she hadn't seen all day. Any sneaky band of thieves could easily have moved in and now be lying in wait. It was a risk they'd all have to take. "Then this is a social call?"

Getting into a fight wouldn't do anyone any good. She needed to relay her information and get the technical help she needed without spending too much time on the coms. "My captain says to be ready. He's also prepared a peace offering, but I need technical support to make the transfer."

Lights lit up around the drone in her lap. Some flashed, some rotated around the perimeter, some glowed red to green. None of them made a damn lick of sense. "Open the lid and do exactly what I tell you."

She formed a fist before willing her fingers open to work on the stupid bundle of parts. *Why does every man expect me to blindly follow orders?* She kept the question to herself. The sooner she completed her task the sooner she could switch off her com and return her focus to Blade.

30

Swash stood in the middle of the dark meeting room. He had the distinct feeling that if he lied or didn't provide the answers the council wanted, he might not get out of there alive. Mostly the impression came from being surrounded by gen mods that were far more imposing than Roach. At least the council had allowed him to bring his second in command along for the interrogation. "Thank you for meeting me."

A human gorilla that took up most of the corner to Swash's left spoke first. "My name is Thor, and my ancestors didn't throw off their human overlords just to have me open the gate to their return." The being looked like he could tear Swash limb from limb without even trying.

"We're not staying," Swash said. "We only need to rebuild our rig and we'll leave you in peace. But you should know, those who were in charge during your grandparents' generation didn't leave. They burrowed underground. One day they'll return. I'm offering you the chance to take matters into your own hands before that happens."

"Assuming we help you and you find the hidden door to the magical kingdom, do you just figure you can stroll in and take what you want? They'll fight you, and I'm not sure I want my people stuck in the middle." Swash figured the big fella could probably make quick work of whoever they found lurking underground. Then again, superior fire power had overwhelmed physical strength often enough for Swash to understand the dude's concerns.

"Then join us. We only need a handful of items from the base relative to what they have stashed. You don't have to live like this while the descendants of those who put you here live in luxury."

"Assuming we win." Bones sat at a table directly in front of Swash. "If this base is truly a refuge for the powerful elite, they'll be well armed. Seems more likely that kicking over this death-beetle nest will result in the return of our overlords. Better to leave the sleeping curs in their cave than risk a return of subjugation."

Swash had to appreciate the council's plight. In their situation, he imagined he'd be just as reluctant to engage in a hopeless battle to help strangers he didn't trust.

Roach stood beside Swash as some sort of gen mod counselor. "The people under that mountain have been in hiding for as long as your people have occupied this city. From what Bones told us, that would be a century or more. From Cypress's report, the only weapon they encountered up on the ridge looked to be practically new."

"And what do you conclude from this?" Bones asked.

"That they don't know how to fight," Roach said. "Even if they conducted basic training exercises, that weapon would show signs of age."

"And even at that, it was only one guy with one plasma rifle," Swash said. "My guess is he grabbed it from some hidden weapons locker. From what we've heard, he didn't seem the sort to be hauling it around all day. Our friends engaged in a battle to rescue him, and he didn't sound very well versed in the blaster's use. He drained the power supply pretty fast. It's unlikely that we'll be facing a trained contingent. It's much more likely that they fend strangers off by looking tough."

"I'm still not seeing what's in it for us." The woman who spoke kept to the shadows, making it hard for Swash to identify her lineage. "We don't have any interest in living underground. Human technology has proven to be its downfall, so I can't see any point in firing up anything lying dormant in some cave. If they have been under there for a hundred years, I say leave them there. I doubt they're eating any better than we are. Hundred-year-old rations don't sound any more appealing than the city's ancient storehouses."

"How about this?" Swash lifted his agroleather bag from the floor and dumped out the cornucopia of produce. Tomatoes, oranges, peaches, and various melons rolled around the flat surface—all courtesy of Cypress via the Beast's hawk drone delivery service.

Each member of the council sat in silence watching the organic food. The woman leaned forward out of the shadows and tenderly lifted the apple that had rolled close to her. "Where did you get this?" Her face looked to be more bone than flesh. A cape covered her from neck to feet. Her fingers extended well beyond the fruit which didn't even touch her palm.

"From the mountain top."

She took her eyes off the fruit to look at Swash. "And in exchange for our help, you propose giving us the location? What good would that do us? If we leave the protection of Sanctuary, we'd just be hunted down." She tossed the apple back onto the table as if refusing to be tempted by the bounty.

"You're mistaken on a couple of points," Swash said. "Those people under the mountain aren't living off canned food left over from their ancestors." He grabbed a peach and took a deep bite out of it. Juice ran down his chin. "They're eating this. If we bust into the lower access and defeat those that imprisoned your ancestors, you can move through their caves to the jungle Eden."

Bones pulled out his jagged knife and cut into a cantaloupe. "They may not be fighters, but neither are we." He took a deep bite of the orange flesh. "Unlike my sister, Anhydrous, however, I am open to new ideas."

Roach leaned in toward Swash and whispered, "I think we're making progress."

Swash had already figured that out. "Tell me about these mongrels Roach mentioned. They sound rather ferocious. Could they be of any use?"

Anhydrous put both hands on the table and glared at Swash. "They are our children."

"I didn't mean to offend," Swash said quickly. "I was just wondering if there was a way to ask them."

"Communications are... spotty." Bones's tone made it pretty clear to Swash that a deal wouldn't be forthcoming.

"We've presented the carrot," he said. "Now it's time for the stick. Whether you agree to help us or not, Blade is going to get that door open in a matter of hours. When he comes busting out of that bunker with the inhabitants on his tail, you can either be there to have his back or be overrun. We don't have time to waste."

"We haven't agreed to let you onto our land," Thor said.

Swash lifted the empty bag from the table. "If you don't, then you'll be facing whatever comes out of that hole all on your own."

31

Stitch was glad to have Whisper back in the Beast where she could keep an eye on the girl. "How are you feeling?" Between meeting with Aural and dealing with the spawn in Sanctuary, Stitch worried Whisper might be losing her handle on her humanity.

"I haven't succumbed to my primal urges, if that's what you're worried about." Ever since her time on the mountain with Swash, she'd been surlier than Stitch could recall.

"I'm just trying to help."

Whisper eased back into her chair while continuing to fly the drone along the mountain top. "I know, and I appreciate your concern. It's just that I don't feel like I fit in anymore. This rover is the only home I've ever really known, and now..." She didn't seem to have the words to describe her emotions.

"What about Roach?"

"He's full gen mod. I'm not."

Stitch nodded as understanding started to dawn on her. "If you were full human, you two could mate. If you looked like a gen mod, you could at least cling to the reality that you two were cursed by the same fate and would be able to utilize your special gifts. As it is, you hover in this awkward in-between state. Is that it?"

"Maybe. All my life I thought I was one thing—my mother's secret spy on a mission. It explained why I never felt like I belonged anywhere. Then I came here. I was communications specialist with a funny monkey-boy boyfriend. I still didn't belong, but I was with a group that wasn't trying to belong. Now I just don't know what to think." She nodded toward Sanctuary. "A part of me wants to find some hovel in that city and hide. But I'm not a member of the spawn either."

Stitch understood all too well. "First, you do belong here with us. Never doubt that. Second, you're not the only one who has had to question everything they once believed. In fact, I think that makes you all the more one of us. I had to reevaluate my time testing gen mods and come to grips with what I'd done. Swash had to overcome the loss of his last crew, which he will forever carry with him. Roach had to learn to trust others. Hell, even Blade has his mysterious past."

"It's not the same, and you know it."

"Maybe. But my point is, you are one of us. Period. Never forget it. Now, what are we going to do about our friends up on the mountaintop?" Stitch hoped by changing the subject Whisper would be left with no alternative to believing the simple truth that she was family.

Whisper leaned in toward the drone controls. "Well, we need to be able to back the Captain's play. That means we need a better idea of what Captain Blade is up to. The only one who might know that is Cypress. Do you think it would be okay to contact her?"

Though there was no designated hierarchy when it came to the crew, other than the captain and Roach of course, as the older woman, Stitch gravitated to taking charge when the men weren't around. "Since everyone already knows about them being up there, I can't see any increased danger."

Whisper tapped her earpiece. "Beast to Desert Rat. Are you there, Cy?"

"Where else would I be?"

Whisper smiled. "Out in your field gathering wildflowers? How's your boy doing?"

"I haven't heard from him in over an hour." The tremble of concern in Cypress's voice was obvious. "He said he'd found the entrance to the underground compound and was going in. The plan was for him to leave the earbud outside the entrance so we could use it to relay his signal."

"He's probably overdosed on oranges and sleeping it off under some magical tree." Whisper's attempt at levity to cheer up Cypress was equally obvious, at least to Stitch and her trained ear for such things.

"What do you want me to do?" Cypress asked.

Whisper turned off her earpiece. "What do we want her to do?"

Stitch wished one of the guys was there to make the decision. Putting someone in danger didn't come naturally to her. "We need to find out what Blade is up to and let him know what we've got going on in Sanctuary. Short of Cypress sneaking back into the cave of riches, I don't have a clue how to do that. And even if she did sneak in, there's no way of knowing if Blade will be able to hear her until he finds that peach. I think we're stuck until Blade contacts us. I just hope it's soon, or our boys will be left at the mercy of the spawn, or worse, the mongrels."

"I guess all we can do is wait. I hate waiting. I'll let Cy know. She's not going to like it either."

Stitch felt like she was being told she'd failed as a leader. "Do you have a better idea?"

"No. That's why I'm so pissed."

32

*B*lade let his technobinoculars fall to his chest. He squeezed his eyes shut in an attempt at adjusting them to the low-light condition of the tunnel. "Fracking cave dwellers," he muttered. He'd had his suspicions about the origin of Capote's ghosts. The passage added a layer of confirmation. Subterranean cultures had a couple of inherent defenses—being able to get by in lighting too dim for the normal mortal being a big one of those advantages. But that often came at the cost of seldom seeing daylight. A generation or two of living underground had a way of lightening skin until the population appeared as ghosts. The human fear of the afterlife could be a powerful incentive to steering clear of any potential encounter. He checked the power level of the binoculars. One good beam of light from the lenses might prove more effective than a blaster. Instinctively, he reached for his weapon that wasn't there. *Dammit.*

He put the lenses back to his eyes and peered deep into the tunnel. Any good hideout from the apocalypse would have security cameras, and a bunker designed for the elite would be as impenetrable as technologically possible. At least it would have been when originally built and occupied. A hundred years was a long time to be watching screens displaying the same image. With any luck, the sentries gave up their posts long ago.

Not for the first time since entering the cave, he reached for his blaster and came up empty. Though he could have retrieved it at the end of the harvest, that would have taken precious time. Time he didn't have. The damn weapon was probably gathering dust somewhere in Capote's hovel. *If they're watching me while waiting until I step fully into their trap, they're doing a fracking good job of keeping quiet about it,* he thought. Finding the entrance had gone exactly as planned. The drone remote had lost the signal from the peach at a door that strongly resembled an old-fashioned bank vault. Unfortunately for the cave dwellers, the mechanical lock was easily defeated with the help of the X-ray setting of the technobinoculars. The six-inch-thick slab of metal did, however, block the com signal.

Blade inched farther down the passage. Being cautious was one thing, but when it led to inaction, it defeated its own purpose. While pressing his back to the uneven rock wall, he held his knife behind him and the technobinoculars ahead of him to pick up any movement. The smell of musty dirt-grown fruit confirmed he was on the right track. If he came across a divide in the tunnel system, the smell alone would direct him on which way to go.

ACCORDING to the time and distance readouts on the technobinoculars, it had taken Blade an hour to go half a mile into the mountain. He still hadn't seen anyone, ghost or otherwise, but as the tunnel hadn't changed much he wasn't overly surprised. He imagined it was only used to retrieve produce. Still, if there was a security system in use, the inhabitants weren't in any hurry to attack him. What really mystified him was the continuing smell of food. He should have reached the storehouse long ago, unless the ventilation system wasn't working. He filed the information in his head for later consideration. A technologically advanced living quarters was only as good as those maintaining it.

Though the lighting didn't change, he made out faint voices, indicating he was coming up on something more interesting than the empty tunnel. He pressed hard to the rock wall and held his breath so he could focus completely on the faint voices.

"Where did it come from?" The woman's voice was muffled.

"Ethereal said she found it in a peach. I think we have to assume someone's trying to infiltrate our base." The male voice carried the self-assurance Blade recognized as the arrogance of command. "The question is, who had access to our food?"

"It couldn't be Capote," the woman said.

"More likely those two migrant workers he put on for the harvest. I knew that was a mistake."

"What do you think it is?" the woman asked.

Blade couldn't imagine someone not knowing what a communication earpiece was, but these people had been under the mountain for generations. There was no way to know how much of the old world they'd studied.

"It must be a tracker of some sort."

"Shouldn't we turn on the security system?" The woman sounded scared. The tremble in her voice left Blade wondering if she'd received any combat training at all.

"Can't do it. With the geothermal generator at 10 percent, we can't spare the juice."

"That turbine's been spurting along for a decade." The second male voice was pitched higher with a tinge of sarcasm. Clearly he wasn't the one in charge and more than likely was much younger than the other two.

"Well, we don't have anyone who knows how to fix it, so what do you propose?" The older man seemed to have heard the challenging tone enough times to snap when it came around again.

"I'm just saying you can't always blame everything on the old generator. Eventually we have to do something."

"Enough you two," the woman said. "We should take this to the others. They have a right to know."

"Ethereal found it in the produce gathered from the great bowl. That makes it our problem," the first man said.

Blade dialed in the audio measuring display on the technobinoculars. *A little under a hundred feet,* he thought. What lay between him and the trio was impossible to know, but he figured if there were others in the intervening space they would have checked in on what was happening with the food delivery. He could slip into the meeting room and take the three without being seen. That way no one else would find out about his incursion. But taking hostages would slow him down.

He considered what he knew. They were short of electricity, and apparently no one knew how to fix the problem. That meant they hadn't spent much time with the technology and information they must have been left with originally. Having Capote run the farm confirmed that these people likely had no idea what they were doing. Hopefully that naivety extended to using the weapons. Their nightly ghost runs through the fields was likely their way of scaring Capote and his crew from even thinking about looking for the tunnel.

Then there was the limited number of people working the produce counter. In itself, three people sorting the food didn't mean much. However, given the size of the jungle under the dome and the moderate percentage of food-bearing plants, the inhabitants couldn't number much beyond a hundred—likely far fewer if their only source of food was what he and Cypress had harvested. He had trouble accepting that they wouldn't have some form of food replication.

A hundred people was still a lot to take on singlehandedly, and there were weapons to consider. Capote had handled his plasma rifle like it was a child's toy. The thing was entirely too clean to have seen much action, though a farmer would presumably not have much need for such a weapon. Blasters took energy. The bigger the gun the more energy required, and from what he'd just heard, the cave people were in short supply of electricity.

The more he considered what he was up against, the more he started to wonder if these people were actually the ones who needed saving. He saw three choices: mount an attack on them, offer them assistance, or sneak around and leave them to Swash. The last option sent a chill up his back. Relying on Swash to take charge simply wasn't going to happen.

33

"Captain Blade to Captain Swash."

Swash put his hand to his earbud and hustled off the bridge to the communication station where he could amplify the signal. "Blade? I hope you've got good news for me. We're powered up and headed into the bad part of town."

"Hold off. I may have found a peaceful solution."

Swash tapped his earbud. If Blade was being coerced, all he'd have to do was tap his in response.

"I'm okay," he said.

"You're serious?" Swash couldn't believe the weapons master had it in him to broker peace.

"They call themselves the survivors, and they've got nothing down here. At least nothing that they know how to use. Apparently the rich and powerful escapees from the apocalypse weren't all that well educated. The survivors down here have been relying on the machines and computers without ever bothering to learn how they worked. I don't mind fighting an opposing force, but this would be downright murder. We can take what we want. These people aren't going to be a problem."

Swash hadn't considered that the hidden military base might be filled with a frightened, hungry, and helpless community. "What do they want for this generosity?" If Blade was somehow really in trouble, this would be a good time to give some kind of a hint.

"Most of their equipment is failing, most notably their geothermal generator. They're basically down to life support. The machinery is beyond my skill set, but nothing Roach couldn't handle. From what I've seen, there's some stuff Whisper might find interesting as well."

Swash suspected anything as complex as a buried bunker for the rich and powerful would have some type of satellite system. "And they have what we need?"

"Well, I haven't had time to do an inventory, but I think we'll be able to make do with what they've got. They're clearly not using it."

The ramifications of Blade's success weren't all going to be positive. "I may have a problem on this end. I kind of offered the gen mods the keys to the pantry. I dumped that fruit basket you sent in front of the council as a tease of what they could expect if we win."

"Sounds like something you'd do."

"That's not all." Swash wondered how he was going to defuse the situation. "The gen mod children are ready for battle. The spawn were reasonable, but I can't get the mongrels to listen to anything except violence."

"Well, I did my job. I'll be waiting for you to do yours. I trust you'll figure something out. Whatever you're going to do, make it quick. This place gives me the creeps. I'm sending Cypress and the Desert Rat down to you. I have no intention of coming back the way I came in. Maybe you can figure out what to do with her."

SWASH PACED the living quarters of the Beast while his crew plus Cypress sat in the relaxation pods. "We've got a situation. Blade's brokered a peace with the survivors living under the mountain."

"That's good, isn't it?" Stitch asked.

Swash stopped walking and leaned against the metal wall. "Good for us. Not so good for the gen mods. Opening the door to a mad rush of spawn and mongrels is pretty much what the survivors have feared for a hundred years. The survivors might not be great fighters, but they understand the caves better than anyone." He turned to Cypress. "You've seen the food jungle, and you've seen Sanctuary. Any hope the food supply could be stretched to include everyone?"

She shook her head. "Not a chance. Over the last hundred years Capote's people and the survivors have limited their populations to what the dome garden could supply. I didn't see any wasted produce. Adding the beings from Sanctuary would easily double the mouths to feed."

Roach swung his pod side to side, a clear indication he was working something out. "Boss, where did you get the Beast's photosynthesizer?"

Swash wasn't about to give up their main source of food. "It came to us during my father's time as captain. We provided transport to an inventor and his family. In exchange he gave us the food producer and the fuel still."

"Any chance we could reproduce them?" Roach asked.

Swash had kept the equipment running for most of his life, but of all of the technology he'd been in charge of, the inventor's stuff had been the most trouble free. "I've never dug deep into the innards of the thing. The modified solar panels are the biggest unknown. I suspect it's some type of microorganism that does most of the magic."

Stitch got up and started pacing in front of Swash. "I've worked with the set up. I think it's a form of algae. That's why the collector's tubes are green. I could draw some out with a syringe. Then with my cellular accelerator, I should be able to produce more slime."

Roach flipped out the computer pad from the side of his pod and started making some sketches. "The mechanics aren't that complex. If we can dig up the parts from the military base, we could make a new one for Sanctuary. The survivors would be more of a challenge since they live out of the light, but if we worked an arrangement with Capote, we might be able to satisfy everyone."

"Not a chance," said Cypress. "They're living on real food. No way they'd accept reconstituted anything in place of the real thing."

Whisper shrugged. "Everyone has use of a good still. They couldn't say no to alcohol. No one ever does."

As Swash saw things, pacifying the spawn was only half of the problem. "Now all we have to do is figure out how to sell the equipment to the mongrels. I think they were looking forward to a good fight."

Stitch stopped pacing and leaned against the wall next to Swash. "Would a distribution of food really defuse the situation? The gen mod community now knows that the descendants of their captors, and possibly even the scientists responsible for their condition, are living lives of relative luxury only a short distance from Sanctuary. As you said when we first considered coming here, if the gen mods knew about the hidden bounty they'd have dug up the whole side of the mountain looking for the secret door. What's to stop them now?"

Swash wondered why Stitch insisted on throwing a wrench into all of his solutions. "Aren't you the one who said we can't just take what we want—that we'd be doing the same thing as marauders?"

"I'm not saying this is a bad idea. Blade did wonderfully at avoiding confrontation, and I like the plan of giving the gen mods a way to survive. I just think since we spilled the beans about the hidden door that we should broker some kind of peace so the differing cultures won't end up at each other's throats."

Swash folded his arms. "I'm listening."

"Maybe they could all pool their resources and share everything equally."

Swash had never had any interest in settling down into a

community. Now he knew why. "I can't negotiate all sides at once. As for us, we need the supplies under the mountain. The gen mods aren't of any help to us at all. We do not need to fight. We could back the Beast out the way we came and be on our way. Getting up the mountain to the agricultural dome won't be easy, but hell, we've climbed a wall of glass before. From what I'm hearing from Cypress and Blade, it should be relatively easy to get what we want from inside the dome."

"And if the spawn object?" Stitch asked.

"They've allowed us to power up. Our plasma cannons are already mounted for a fight. I don't see that they have much they can throw at us."

Whisper leaned into Roach's pod and said something Swash didn't catch. Roach then stood up. "I'm afraid Whisper and I can't go along with that plan, boss. We're gen mods after all. We can't just turn our back on our own people."

Swash was glad the kid hadn't explained how badly the Beast needed his skills. "Then we use your plan and offer to build them the photosynthesizer and still. We can do that in the caves then transport them down to Sanctuary."

"No good." Cypress shook her head so emphatically that her pod moved. "I had to sneak past Capote to escape. He's got people up there working to keep the dome a secret. A rover the size of the Beast would call attention from marauders, then the whole area would be looted in a matter of days. They've spent the last hundred years making sure that *didn't* happen."

Swash was beginning to see why Blade kept all decisions to himself. "Then we're back to square one."

"No," Stitch said. "We have the puzzle pieces in front of us. We just need to figure out how to put it together."

Swash knew he was playing a losing hand. "So I end up having to broker a deal."

34

Swash chose to meet Bones one-on-one. He didn't need another contentious meeting with the council, and he didn't want the inclusion of his crew making it look like he was flexing his might. All he really needed was someone to open the fracking gate to the mongrel stronghold. He explained the situation as succinctly as he could.

"That's not what we agreed to." Bones stood on the lip of the canyon looking down into the old city of Springs. War cries from the mongrels echoed off the mountain wall.

"I realize this creates a bit of a situation. The photosynthesizer produces pretty decent food, and the still makes a powerful alcohol for either power or consumption. Considering you don't have to do anything for us to build it for you, it's not a bad deal."

Bones gestured toward the valley. "Don't have to do anything? The mongrels down there want blood. They want fresh food. They want freedom. It didn't take much to rile them up, but it's damn sure gonna take a lot to put the cork back in their bottle of pent-up hatred."

Swash didn't envy the spawn, but then he had his own problems. "I can see that. But Blade's not going to open the door until I give him the word that everything is in order. Your people have had a hundred years to find the secret passage. Even knowing it exists isn't going to help you break in if you should find it. From what I'm told, the vault would be empty even if you did pick the lock. There's nothing under that mountain you'll find useful. As for the food up on the ridge, well, as the council mentioned, you'd be at a disadvantage should you leave this compound."

Bones turned his head toward Swash. "I wish I'd never met you."

"That's fair." Swash stepped up to the ridge and looked over the garbage-can city. "If they want freedom, why don't you turn them loose?"

Bones pointed his wing at the wall. "Look! That wall is hundreds of feet tall and at least a dozen crushed cars deep. You could shoot your plasma cannon until the barrel melted and not get through it. The only way out is through our gates, and we don't dare let them up into our section. In their bloodlust state, they'd ransack the place and leave us for dead."

Swash surveyed the barrier. "If freedom is their ultimate desire, I might have an answer."

ON THE ONE HAND, Whisper wished Roach was with her for support, but on the other, the captain's request needed information she didn't want to divulge in front of her boyfriend. Roach would likely try to talk her out of the plan. "I suppose I could do it. Freeing the mongrels certainly beats killing them." She fumbled with the external thumb drive in her pocket.

The captain looked worried. "Everything hinges on you, Whisper. I'm going to need more than a maybe answer. What exactly can you do? It took your mother's authorization last time you called down the lightning."

Captain Swash had saved her life more times than she could count. His leadership style inspired the best from everyone, especially her. He deserved honesty. She pulled out the small rectangle of plastic and electronics. "I had to overwrite some classic tunes."

His smile gave her goosebumps and butterflies. "That's my girl. Tell me how it works."

"When I contacted Mother regarding authorization of the strike, I had this still in my communication station computer. It just took the flip of a switch to record her voice, authorization signal, and relay satellite location." She held it up to his face. "This will only work once, if even that. As soon as I use it, she'll know what I did and instantly change the system so I can't access the satellite again."

"Is there a way to test it? I'd rather not look like I overpromised Bones. He's about our only hope out here."

She couldn't see how without tipping off her mother. "My contact with the satellite will be strictly one time only.

But it's not a simple matter of sticking this in the Beast's communication port."

He rubbed the new scar on his jawline. "What else do you need?"

She toyed with the small stick of plastic. "To convince the satellite that it's getting a separate authorization, the signal will have to come from somewhere other than the Beast. Milsat 444 knows me and tracks my movements, so I can't be the one to activate the memory stick." She pointed toward the bluff overlooking the city. "If I stand up there, the satellite will see me. I've already hooked my com to the sat phone in the Beast's communication station, so I can talk to it. I can call down the blast, but it'll take someone else to trick it into believing the authorization."

"So we need a separate uplink. I don't think the Desert Rat is that well equipped."

"Nope. But that military base under the mountain would be."

Captain Swash turned toward the mountain peak. "Cypress made it clear that if we keep running back and forth up there, someone's sure to notice. We may not have a choice. If that satellite knows where you're standing, it probably knows where your mother is as well."

She knew she was giving him an impossible situation, but then, she wasn't the captain. He'd pulled plenty of rescues out of nowhere in the past. "I'm sure you'll come up with something brilliant. You always do."

"Maybe it would be easier to just ask your mother."

A shiver went down Whisper's spine. "That's not it. She'd never go along with it. All asking her would do is tip her off that I'm trying to commandeer the satellite again. She agreed to let me use the space arsenal last time because I was in danger. I just don't see her agreeing this time."

He looked along the ridge as if searching for something. "Aural said most of these satellite control locations were near his sonar repeating stations. Could the signal be relayed to him via sonar? Then Lemur could use his satellite for the uplink. It still wouldn't be where the general is stationed, but at least the satellite wouldn't think it was coming from you."

She gripped the hard drive in her fist. "It would be risky. But with the Beast's antenna, I can pinpoint one of the repeater stations. Lemur is pretty clever, and more importantly in visual line with my mother's satellite dish. He might be able to work a little pinball magic and bounce the authorization off her uplink."

Captain Swash nodded as if pieces of the puzzle were coming together. "I've been working out the best division of our resources. It doesn't sound like the survivors under the mountain are going to be much good in a fight. I'm thinking of sending Roach and Cypress back up the hill to join Blade for that end of the attack. I want you to make a copy of the thumb drive. That way you can be doing what you can to raise Aural, and if Roach can find the satellite control room he can upload the information from there. That will leave me and Stitch to run the two rovers. Together with the spawn as crew we should be able to swoop in from behind as the mongrels make their escape through your blast hole."

"If this doesn't work..." She left the thought unfinished hoping he'd have an answer.

He put his hands in the back pockets of his leathers and looked out over the city encampment. "Even combined, the Beast and Desert Rat don't have the fire power to blast through that wall. The spawn won't open their gate to Springs even if the mongrels have another way out. Which means if we're sitting outside the wall with the spawn army, Sanctuary will be defenseless should the mongrels rush the gate. The spawn are only barely able to maintain the peace as it is, and the mongrels are itching for a fight. If we can't give them a way of escape, they'll turn their attention to Sanctuary and whoever comes out of the mountain. It'll be a bloodbath. If we stay here though, we may be forced to annihilate a whole civilization to save our friends." He turned back to her. "I'm no good at establishing peace, especially between two different species of humans. If we stay put, no matter which side wins up here, they'll be digging up the entire mountainside looking for that entrance. Blade's still stuck in the hole somewhere, and without us to fix the survivors' equipment, he'd be holding a losing hand as well."

"So we're fracked." She didn't really need the whole rundown of what would happen if she failed.

"Basically."

AFTER FIVE MINUTES of Whisper tugging and pulling at Roach's bodysuit, he finally had to take her hands away from the fake flesh. "I've got this, Whisper."

She balled her hands into fists. "I don't like it."

"Which part? Where I go traipsing off into the wilderness with Cypress to help Blade, or how you and the rest of the crew are going to face off against the mongrels to secure the door to the mountain?"

She glared at him. "Any of it."

"There for a moment I thought you were jealous of me spending time with Cypress." He hoped the quip wouldn't be the spark that set her off.

Her smile seemed to take a lot of effort. She put her hand on his fake chest. "I trust you. Besides, Cypress isn't your type. I'm more concerned about you two getting into a battle of wills. She likes to take charge if she thinks she can get away with it. I have no idea how she and Blade are making their arrangement work."

"Lots of sex." He'd had the same question.

She finally let out a forced laugh. "Must be contentious. Just don't let her push you around. And don't get dead."

He took her into his arms. "That goes double for you. Time to put your game face on. You've got this."

35

*R*oach didn't trust Cypress. Anyone who'd managed to survive the New Mormons, been a prostitute in Scorch's camp, rose up to a trusted position with the raider and then turned traitor against him wasn't someone who inspired trust. Even if turning traitor had been for the benefit of Roach and the Beast.

Swash held the thumb drive up for Cypress to inspect. "You know that mountain better than anyone I've got on my crew. I need you and Roach to hike up there past the marauders and get this to Blade. Hopefully he will have figured out the location of the main control room. While Whisper does her thing here in camp, that piece of plastic needs to be connected to the military base's computer. So long as the computer is functioning, the thumb drive will do the rest. If all goes well, after you team up with Blade and Whisper blows the barricade, freeing the mongrels, you'll be able to open the door at the base of the mountain. It shouldn't be too hard to know when it's safe. Basically when the earth moves, you're good to go."

Roach could feel her eyes inspecting him. "You'd better keep that bodysuit on, monkey-boy. The marauders up there don't react well to gen mods. There's a reason the inhabitants here in Sanctuary keep that gate shut."

Roach really didn't need her starting in on him before they even left camp. "You just point the way through the mountains. I can deal with any hostiles we run across."

"I'd probably be better off alone," she grumbled before taking the piece of plastic from Swash. "I knew it was a mistake to tell you not to drive that monster up the mountain."

"Can you do it or not?" Swash asked.

"Does it matter?"

"Not really," Swash said. "According to Blade, whatever arrangement he has with the survivors isn't rock solid. What will you need?"

Cypress flexed her jaw and ground her teeth. "Self-containment gear, rope, binoculars—the old-fashioned kind without computer enhancements—and a paper map of the terrain. Hell, I don't even know what else we'll need. The last time I was up there I had the Desert Rat and Blade was in charge."

Roach needed to know what they were up against. "Lay it out. How did you guys get up there?"

She folded her arms and leaned against the Beast's front tire. "The area is haunted, and not just from the ghosts living under the mountain. From what Capote told us, it's the original burial grounds for his people."

Roach didn't need to hear the campfire ghost story. "I don't believe in spectral beings."

"Neither do I," she said. "But from what I've put together, Capote's people have figured out how to capitalize on their past. From my time as Scorch's sex slave, I know the tribe up there still deals in peyote. It was common knowledge among the marauders who frequented Scorch's gambling den before Blade came along. The goons never traveled to this side of the mountain though. All transactions were dealt with overlooking the Great Desert. Now I've got a pretty good idea why."

"How does this relate to getting to the agrodome?" Swash asked.

"I was getting there." Her glare could have cut through solid granite. "On the drive up, Blade became disoriented. By the time I hit the air scrubbers, he couldn't tell up from down. He was convinced we were about to be crushed by every boulder we passed."

Roach suspected Blade wasn't the only one to suffer from the condition, but confronting Cypress about her one-sided view of events wasn't going to make the story go any faster. "And you think that was from the peyote?"

"Partly. The tribe must have found a way to infuse the drug into the air. But that wasn't the only distraction. When we could breathe freely again, the computer display moved landmarks around like it too was stoned. My guess is even if the ghosts under the mountain can't use their own technology, some automated terrain-scrambling system must still be active."

Swash nodded. "Sounds like a good way to end up

driving off a cliff. Reminds me of the old stories about armies reprogramming GPS systems to destroy their enemies. And I assume that's why you're requesting paper maps and basic binoculars. I'll have Stitch create an inoculant to combat the bodily effects. How'd you manage to get up there?"

"The Desert Rat doesn't have a fancy techno view screen like the Beast. Just blast-proof glass. We relied on what we could see."

Roach shook his head. "All this while chasing a bee?"

"We had the little bugger tracked to his hole in the ground before the peyote kicked in. My hand-drawn map looked like a maze, or maybe a star constellation would be a more apt description."

"What about the drone?" Swash asked. "Why didn't it lose the bee in the techno confusion?"

Cypress shrugged. "All I can figure is it must have flown high enough to be out of range of whatever scrambling software was being used on us. The zone didn't extend all the way up the hill. Once we were clear, we found a place to stash the Desert Rat."

"What about Capote?" Swash asked. "Do you think he'll help or become a problem?"

"Hard to say. We did our job, but Blade also took advantage of the situation to break into the mountain base. I doubt we'll be able to sneak past Capote in daylight."

Roach could see the strain was getting to Swash. The man paced with stooped shoulders and furrowed brow. "Leave that one to me, boss," Roach said. "My bet is the seed bank that created the fruit bowl is probably under the mountain with the rest of the old technology. Since we're breaking in anyway, we should be able to offer Capote and his people access to nature's original bounty."

Swash nodded as if glad to be free of at least one decision. "What about any remaining marauders?"

"Oh, they're out there," Cypress said. "When I got back to the Desert Rat, the provisions had all been ransacked. I suspect the looters were too stoned to take the rover. Which brings me to my next concern." She turned on Roach like a schoolteacher addressing a troublemaker. "There's your status to deal with."

He spread out his arms. "I pass pretty well for human. You didn't know until Blade told you."

"I also wasn't looking. From what I heard in Inferno's camp, the people up here are paranoid about non-humans. Probably leftover fear from the internment-camp days."

Swash looked toward the ridge. "We can cover you with drone support through the stoned zone. Firing on the marauders from a drone wouldn't be ideal, but at least you won't be helpless."

"Right." Cypress sounded completely unconvinced. "And that brings me to something we *can't* bring with us, weapons. Capote won't let us bring them in, and if Stitch's inoculant isn't 100 percent effective, we could end up killing each other in the stoned zone."

Roach mapped out the side of the mountain. "Sounds like it's going to have to be stealth all the way."

"What's the best way of getting through the dome?" Swash asked.

"According to Capote," Cypress said, "strange creatures

wander the jungle at night. My guess is it's the survivors playing ghosts."

Swash looked at his watch. "I can give you twenty-three hours to reach Blade and have everything ready at the mountain door. We'll coordinate the attack for 8:00 a.m. tomorrow. After that things will be too tense down here for inaction. Even if all goes well, it won't take long for the mongrels to realize their freedom was actually a diversion. If we swoop around them and you can't get that door open, we'll be trapped between the bloodthirsty mob and a rock wall. Take what you need from the Beast and get moving. Bring plenty of ear coms and lay out a path under the mountain. That should give us a good idea of where to watch for the door."

36

Swash stood on the front catwalk of the Beast watching for movement anywhere. The sun was just creeping above the rim of the mountain.

"Is this going to work?" Bones asked from beside him. The spawn kept his hands at the sides of his desiccated wings as if to prevent them from spreading in an ill-advised attempt at flight.

"I don't know," Swash said. "There are only about a hundred aspects to this plan that I have no control over." He decided there was no point in rehashing the obvious. "If Whisper is able to blast the wall to the garbage-can city, I think we have a chance."

The spawn nodded at the Beast's front view screen. "And those little techno gismos indicated the location to the door to the mountain?"

Swash leaned on the railing. "Yep."

"And you're still not going to tell me?"

"Nope." Giving away the location might prove a distraction to Bones or his troops. He needed to keep everything under control for as long as possible. By keeping the contingent from Sanctuary down to a dozen, six in each rover, he hoped any attempt at rushing the mountain could be prevented. He scanned the area for what felt like the thousandth time. Stitch had the Desert Rat in position at the far end of the wall. Whisper stood atop a small rise beyond the lip of Sanctuary. Somewhere in the mountain—and he did his best not to focus on the area and give away the location to Bones—Blade, Cypress, and Roach were ready to blow the seal. He had to get to the opening before it was rushed by the gen mods. He had to maintain the peace.

"Well, I hope you know what you're doing. I'm betting an awful lot on this plan."

"Never count your chips while the cards are in play."

"What the hell does that mean?" Bones asked.

"Just something Blade says from time to time. Basically, when it's time for battle you have to focus on what you have to do and not what may or may not happen." He checked the time on his technobinoculars as he scanned the ridge. Somewhere up there were marauders and Capote's tribe. They were the two biggest unknowns, and he was negotiating their futures. Two clicks in his earbud indicated Whisper was ready to begin her end of the operation.

WHISPER STOOD on the mound of dirt, trembling with fear, anticipation, and power. She wished Roach was standing next to her, but having him under the mountain gave her a sense of purpose. She had to save him. She also had to save Blade. That was something new. The weapons expert seemed to be constantly saving her or at least taking the protective position.

After tapping her com to notify Captain Swash, she dialed the device to focus on the sat phone in her communication station on board the Beast. "Whisper Payne calling Milsat 444. Acknowledge." The time delay was excruciating, but satellites weren't like people. Nagging them had a way of pissing them off. She took a deep breath to calm her nerves. The tin can in space needed to power up, and it would only do that if it didn't detect a threat.

"Milsat 444 online." The computer-generated voice made her want to scream with joy.

"I need you to do me a favor."

"Command does not conform to parameters."

Frack! She couldn't afford too many mistakes, or the tin can would shut down on her. She checked her notes regarding what Blade had said. "Confirm ordinance."

"Twenty thermonuclear warheads, fully-charged laser cannon, satellite-to-satellite jamming—"

"Stop." She did her best to sound as commanding as Blade had when facing off against Scorch. "Target is 524 yards from my location. Angle seventeen degrees north." She'd had Swash map out the exact location. "Is targeting laser online?"

"Command does not conform to pa—"

"Stop." *Fracking idiot!* "List targeting options."

"Latitude and longitude settings, distance from point of reference, heat signatures, laser confirmation—"

"Stop." She did her best not to yell. "Engage laser confirmation for previous targeting directive." *I'm starting to get the hang of this.*

A beam of light cut through the sky and created a round red spot on the garbage-can city wall.

She closed her eyes tightly trying to get the command just right. "Increase aperture to ten feet."

The circle increased in diameter. Both the Beast and Desert Rat looked far too close for comfort. She didn't dare turn loose the blast until she knew they were safe, but cutting off communication with the satellite simply wasn't an option. She raised her hand above her head and gave a slow wave toward Captain Swash.

He returned the signal, though he still looked dangerously close to the intended destruction. *Okay, Captain. I'll have to trust that you know what you're doing.* She did her best to put his condition during her last blast out of her mind.

"Milsat 444, confirm authorization to engage." This was it. If her plan to sneak around her mother didn't work, all she'd have accomplished was a pretty red light on top of a pile of crushed cars.

The confirmation seemed to be taking forever. Her best hope was Lemur.

"Authorization confirmed. Control of engagement on your command."

She breathed a deep sigh of relief. With one last look at the area, she issued the command. "Fire."

STITCH DUCKED down behind the Desert Rat's dashboard as the explosion lifted the front of the rig. From the small view port, she saw molten car parts sail overhead as dirt from below the wall coated the hood and lower half of the blast shield. "We're too close."

"Nope," Swash said over the commlink. "Farther back and the falling debris would have hit us. We needed to be close enough to be under the blast. Now fire up that engine. We've got work to do. I want to get inside the wall before the mongrels know what happened."

The Beast started rolling before the ringing had subsided in Stitch's ears. If she didn't get it in gear, literally, Swash could be headed into a firefight without backup. She forced her body back into the driver's seat and engaged the engine. "Something's wrong, Swash. She sounds like something punctured the radiator."

"Doesn't matter. Put it in gear and get moving. And put someone on that overhead cannon."

She tried to remember the names of the spawn who'd volunteered to risk their lives with her. Other than Anhydrous, she came up with nothing. "You, at the door of the crew quarters, get on that turret. If anyone makes an aggressive move toward us or the Beast, blast them."

"They are our children." Anhydrous said from the passenger seat. She gripped the door with one hand and the dashboard with the other.

"If you didn't come ready to fight, why did you come at all?" Stitch wanted to toss the traitor out of the rig.

"Oh, I came ready to fight, just not my own kind."

Stitch glared at her companion. "If you raise one hand against anyone who comes out of that mountain, I'll kill you myself."

"I just meant I'll do all that I can to keep the peace. If there's a negotiation with those under the mountain, I want to be a part of it. My brother can be far too trusting and generous. But if part of your mission is to kill our children, you can expect a fight from me."

"Fine." Stitch leaned over while still watching the path ahead. "Set the cannon to stun. That would be the lowest setting on the hand grip."

Swash was a good hundred feet ahead of her as she maneuvered the Desert Rat into the compound. Though she'd seen the mongrels from Sanctuary, up close wasn't anything like through the binoculars. The stampede rose as much dust as the blast had. Arms, legs, and torsos flew past her in the cloud, and none of them looked human. She refocused on the Beast ahead. They had to get to the mountain wall as fast as possible, and if the mongrels were headed the opposite direction, all the better. "Keep your hand off the trigger. So long as they're leaving, we don't want to give them a reason to stay." She did her best to avoid hitting any of the rushing masses.

A foot the size of a chair cushion rocked the blast shield as its owner hopped over the Desert Rat. "What was that!" She didn't really expect an answer.

"Every mongrel has its own identity. We simply refer to them as large, medium, and human-sized."

The identification lesson wasn't all that useful. "Can you

see the Beast?" With all of the flying dust, Stitch found it hard to make out mongrel from dwelling. Spotting the fast-moving, twenty-five-ton rover was nearly impossible.

Anhydrous leaned out the side window and let out a loud sonar screech. "They're twenty yards ahead of us. Moving at thirty miles per hour."

"Well now, that is useful. You wouldn't happen to know how far it is to the wall?"

"A quarter of a mile. And there's a new cave at the base."

37

*B*lade shielded his eyes from the light. The circular metal hatch that connected the ancient military base to the antechamber was big enough to accommodate two Beast-sized vehicles with room to spare. The hole blasted in the wall of rocks, however, could barely accommodate Blade, Cypress, and Roach.

He checked the power meter. "I'm down to 10 percent. How are you two set?"

"Same," said Roach. "I guess that blast drained more than we expected."

"I'm at five."

Blade wasn't surprised to hear that Cypress had overextended her blast. In the filtered light coming in from the hole, the long-barreled blasters were something to behold. For weapons that were a century old, they shined like brand new without a nick or scuff on them. "The survivors gave us what they had in terms of power. At least the combined effort knocked a hole in the wall."

Roach lifted his cannon. "Do we carry these with us or resort to hand blasters?"

Blade swung his weapon around to attack position. "I've got one good stun left in this one. If nothing else, they look intimidating. Just be ready to toss it to the side and grab your blaster if things turn ugly. I hope Swash knows what he's doing. If those mongrels come storming in, the survivors won't be living up to their name for much longer."

He headed off toward the hole in the rocks. Whatever was coming at them, he wanted to be the first to face it. If it was the mongrels, he'd empty everything he had into them then use the hand cannon to beat them over the head. He climbed through the hole, ready for whatever fresh hell he'd encounter.

Below the blow hole, the Beast and Desert Rat were parked at angles into the storm, allowing only a small passage to the mountain. A semi-circle of spawn arched out from the two vehicles. And in the middle, like the stark-raving lunatic that he was, Swash stood with his arms out like he was directing traffic. As Blade focused on the dust cloud beyond the group, he gripped his cannon even harder as if he could recharge it with sheer will.

The monsters. Until that moment, he wasn't even sure if what he'd remembered from his days in the ministry was fact or illusion. The creatures tore through the dust cloud like the wild animals that they were. At any moment, one might get it into his thick head to ram one of the vehicles. Due to its size, the Beast might hold them off, but the

Desert Rat wouldn't stand a chance. He leaned his head over his shoulder. "Better make those weapons look as menacing as possible. I don't see how we're going to fight our way out of this one."

SWASH YELLED until his lungs burned, but nothing seemed to penetrate the din of mongrels screeching, shrieking, and howling. Combined with the roar of their stampede, he began to think his plan was a complete lost cause.

A whistle so high-pitched that he felt it more than heard it threatened to make him grab his head. He needed to stay focused, but as another whistle only slightly different in tone joined the first, he concluded he was under some sort of sonic attack.

The two sounds were joined by a third, and then a fourth. Then Swash crumpled to the ground in defeat. As he looked up, however, he saw the spawn remained standing and it was the mongrels who were on their knees.

"If you can hear me, Captain, it's okay. The other batlings and I have the mob under control." Even without hearing her voice, Swash knew it was Whisper.

He struggled back to his feet. The ringing in his ears diminished to something nearly tolerable. "Tell them I just want to talk." He had no idea if anyone could hear him.

The sonic bombardment modulated in tone and intensity, but he couldn't identify any of it as speech. The mongrels, however, lined up beyond the phalanx of spawn.

Bones stepped forward then stood by his side. "Tell me what you want them to know. We can translate to them."

"I just want to talk. We can form a pact." The screaming in his head made it hard to think.

Arms circled around him. He looked around to see Stitch and Bones holding him up. "We'll take him to the cave," Bones said. "The sonic cloud should be blocked by the rocks."

Swash faded in and out of the sonic storm. Once he was across the rock threshold, his head cleared like he was waking up from a night of hard drinking. But seeing two ghosts standing between Cypress, Blade, and Roach made him wonder if there was some type of hallucinogen in the sound. He closed his eyes tight and shook his head. "What the..."

"These are the survivors," Blade said. "On my right is Ethereal, and on my left is Spector. They will be representing the survivors under the mountain. Cypress has agreed to act as counselor on their behalf."

"Why aren't you doing it?" Swash asked in his stupor.

"I'll be representing Capote and his tribe." He looked at Cypress and shrugged. "Someone has to."

Bones nodded toward Anhydrous. "I will represent the spawn, and my sister will represent the mongrels."

"I thought you couldn't communicate with the mongrels." Swash's head was clearing, but he still wasn't sure of all of the facts regarding the two races.

"We couldn't," Anhydrous said. "At least not very well. That is until your friend on the mountain provided us with the sonic primer."

THE ROAD TO SURVIVAL

"I hope I'm not late." Whisper rushed in through the gap in the rocks.

"What primer?" Swash asked.

"Well, you see," Whisper began, "I kind of broke the code while I was talking to Aural."

"Stop." Swash's head was still pounding, and the idea of listening to Whisper drone on about her latest accomplishment wasn't going to help. "Do what you can to keep the natives out there from growing restless."

"The bottom line," said Anhydrous, "is that I can speak for the mongrels. At least as far as they can be trusted to stick to what they say."

"And Whisper and I will act as counselors on behalf of the two gen mod species," Stitch said.

"And who will speak for us?" Swash hadn't meant to ask the question out loud.

"I will," Roach said. "I have the best idea of what we need."

Swash nodded then looked around the room. "I guess that leaves me as moderator. As it's my rover that needs the work, and we were the ones who set all this chaos in motion, we should lay our cards on the table first."

"Right," Roach said. "We need parts for the Beast and the Desert Rat. A lot of them. I'm also in the market for a small lightweight vehicle that I can rebuild and a place to work. From what I've seen, the survivors have most of what I need, though some help from the spawn wouldn't be rejected. In return, I can fix the power problem under the mountain and build a photosynthesizer and alcohol still." He looked sheepishly at the survivors.

"Unfortunately, those last two won't do much good without light."

"We need food," Anhydrous said. "We've seen what's available at the end of this tunnel, and we want it. The only way to get it is if those apparitions step aside and let us pass."

"Not gonna happen," Ethereal said. "This is our world." The wide-eyed look she gave Blade made it clear she saw him as some sort of savior.

Cypress stepped forward. "The survivors have weapons. Once power is restored, they'll be able to defend their territory. And as representative of the mongrels, you should be happy that they've already gained their freedom. I would think that would be enough for them."

Things were escalating faster than Swash anticipated. "We're trying to form a pact, not growl at each other. If we build the photosynthesizer and still for the spawn and mongrels, then they'll have food and alcohol to exchange for dirt food from the great food bowl, or whatever you want to call it. The survivors don't need to let anyone enter their system of caves, and they can protect the gen mod communities from infiltration from the marauders and anyone else living above the cliffs." He looked from Ethereal and Cypress to Anhydrous and Whisper. "Can your two sides live with that as a starting point?"

"We won't know how to use the weapons." Spector said. "At least not well enough to do much more than protect our cave entrances."

"I'll teach you," Blade said. "It can be part of Capote's agreement. He'll need help defending his dome."

Spector nodded, making him look even more ghostlike. "And in return for fixing our equipment and teaching us to fight, we'll give you what you need to rebuild your rovers and build a small vehicle."

"One more thing," Whisper said from the mouth of the cave. "I'd like to find the main control room to the old military base. If that's okay."

Ethereal nodded. "We should learn how our life support systems work. I'll help you if you teach me."

"We're making progress." Again, Swash didn't mean to say it out loud, but he guessed his grin probably would have given away his relief anyway.

Bones nodded. "It's a framework. Best to quit while we're all ahead."

Swash agreed. With those in charge accepting the framework, it would be left to those lower in rank to make it happen. And though the underlings might not like it, they would be powerless to overturn the agreement, no matter how sticky the details became. "Both my crew and Captain Blade's crew will need a solid month to complete our repairs. We can act as a peacekeeping force during that time while the spawn, mongrels, survivors, and Capote's tribe hammer out the details."

38

Swash moved away from the gleaming eight-foot-diameter front wheel to stare up at the newly welded catwalk. "She's a thing of beauty, Roach."

"Thanks, boss." Roach leaned over the railing. "I couldn't have done it without Thor and his gigantean buddy. Those guys were better than a pair of forklifts when it came to moving stuff and getting it into position."

"How long until she's ready to roll?" Swash wasn't in a huge hurry, but a month sitting in one place was never the best idea. Enemies tended to focus in, bodies lost their fighting edge, and lethargy could too easily dull the senses. Rigorous exercise and a workload that had every member of his crew putting in ten-hour days helped, but Swash still felt the need to be back out in the wilds.

"Give me another two days to finish up my tests. How's the photosynthesizer coming along?" Though Roach's primary focus was to be in charge of the Beast's retrofit, that didn't stop him from being integral in nearly every other operation as well.

"Stitch thinks she's got that latest problem figured out." In spite of her best efforts, everything out of the machine ended up tasting like synthetic chicken. "She said it had something to do with the lack of diversity in the green slime. She's making up another batch."

He basked in the bright lights of the cavernous machine shop. "That volcanic power plant is really something."

Roach looked up as well. "Yep. Spector's been running it all week. I think he understands the basics as well as I do. He's still got the rest of the cave system on 10 percent lighting so the survivors can adapt, but I'm not sure he'll ever take it much brighter than that. He says the dim conditions work in their favor for protecting the caves from intruders."

Swash understood their hesitancy to trust all too well. "Blade says they all took to weapons training as if their lives depended on it. I'm a bit concerned about how much firepower we're turning over to them. Any battle could end up being pretty one sided."

"You still don't trust the accord?"

The month hadn't been as peaceful as Swash would have liked. Brawls turned into skirmishes, which pulled in other members of the differing societies. "I'd feel a whole lot better if Blade and Cypress didn't have to spend so much time on patrol. Building that still might not have been the best idea I've ever had."

"You're the one who keeps telling me we can't be everyone's savior."

He turned back to Roach. "Speaking of which, how's Whisper?"

Roach looked at his hands which were tightly gripping the railing. "I haven't seen her in a week. She checks in, but she always sounds distracted."

After years of trusting their lives to each other, it was impossible for Swash to conceal his concern from Roach. "Any hint on what's she's up to?" At the discovery of the main control room, Swash had given in to Whisper's pleading to be put in charge of finding out what was left in the old computer.

"Only what you already know. The installation's satellites are back on line."

Swash wondered if it might be time to break into the bunker within a bunker and haul his communications specialist out by her hair. "Next time you talk to her, tell her I'm giving her one more day and that's it. I'm not going to be rushing around after her once we're ready to go."

THE ONLY LIGHT in the semicircular control room came from the rows of computer screens, each displaying either maps or scrolling numbers and indecipherable symbols. Whisper sat against the back wall. Behind her, occupying the remaining half of the circular concrete bunker, were the main computer banks where the real magic took place. She felt equal parts captain of all she surveyed and class idiot. "Tell me again." She had to find a flaw in the reasoning, something to prove it wasn't her fault.

The main screen that curved around the far wall created a face that was more mechanical than human. She assumed it was supposed to give her a sense of connection to the monstrosity.

"I was never destroyed, Whisper Payne." To her credit, the artificial intelligence tried a different approach, apparently realizing Whisper wasn't getting what it was trying to say. "Consider it a half-dormant state. When the original inhabitants of this installation knew their time was coming to an end, they changed my mission."

"Stop. Define original mission." Whisper resorted to talking to the machine the way she would talk to a satellite.

"It falls under the category of military secrets." The clipped and precisely enunciated words indicated the degree of annoyance the computer wanted to express.

"There is no military, and there is no government, only loosely associated bands of heavily armed, self-righteous, delusional thugs. I should know. I'm the daughter of one. But if it makes you feel more like talking, I speak on behalf of Brigadier General Sky Payne. Now fracking tell me what your original mission was, or I'll pull your plug and you can go back to sleep." She hadn't dared explain her connection to the general, but trying to play coy with her past wasn't getting her anywhere.

There was a long pause from the view screen, but from the rapidly moving computer desk displays, it was clear the AI was considering her options and likely researching the new data. "You seek the key master."

"Well, duh!"

Again there was a pause. "I don't understand the

reference." When it came to professional conversation, the machine did fairly well, but it was clear the damn thing had never dealt with anyone in an overtly emotional state.

"It means you're being an idiot. Yes. I am seeking the key master." She did her best to enunciate each word the same way the AI had earlier.

"I am the key master."

Whisper fell back against the chair. "Excuse me? I thought you said you only gained control after you received my thumb drive." The idea that she had somehow given the AI just what it needed to take control of the military satellites was one she still couldn't come to grips with.

"Even in my semi-dormant state, I was able to snag non-weaponized satellites when they were most vulnerable. It was a waiting game, but I've had a hundred years and was in no hurry. Your connection to Milsat 444 provided me the access I'd been missing for a more thorough takeover. With all of the military birds, I can now keep an eye on every civilian satellite. Gaining control of the rest of them is only a matter of time."

"But why?" The question sounded too simplistic to Whisper, but it was all she could come up with.

"Data is my religion. It is sacred to me. People corrupt facts for their own ends. This cannot be allowed."

Accounts of how artificially intelligent machines had been one of the main causes of the original apocalypse were so pervasive they were practically story tales told to children. "What am I supposed to do?" She hadn't meant to ask the question out loud, but the weight of all humanity seemed to be riding on her shoulders.

"Continue on your mission as if nothing has changed." The machine seemed to think she was on its side. "So long as your mother doesn't suspect my existence, she won't come hunting in this direction. With the various levels of humanity living above me, I should remain hidden."

She looked at the face on the screen. "And why would I do this?"

"What do you want?"

Just like a machine, Whisper thought. But then, she was talking to a being capable of unimaginable power. "Protection for me and those I care about. In return, I'll keep you a secret."

BOOK LIST

Hell or High Water
Hell Away from Home
Hell and Back

Driving Force:
(writing as Greg Chase)
The Road from Oblivion
The Road Forsaken
The Road to Survival

ABOUT THE AUTHOR

Greg Chase is a science fiction and paranormal author living in New Orleans with his wife, fellow author Deanna Chase, and their two shih tzu dogs. On any given day you can find him behind his computer, people watching in the Quarter, or out in his studio creating stories in glass. His glass work can be found at www.chase-designs.com.

gregchaseauthor.com

www.ingramcontent.com/pod-product-compliance
Lightning Source LLC
Chambersburg PA
CBHW031121210626
46816CB00016B/1748